Books are to be returned on or before
the last date below

■- FEB 2011

D0541358

The Runaway

ANGELA MCALLISTER

Illustrated by Peter Bailey

Orion
Children's Books

First published in Great Britain in 2009
by Orion Children's Books
a division of the Orion Publishing Group Ltd
Orion House
5 Upper St Martin's Lane
London WC2H 9EA
An Hachette UK company

1 3 5 7 9 10 8 6 4 2

A catalogue record for this book is available
from the British Library.

ISBN 978 1 84255 599 6

Typeset by Input Data Services Ltd, Bridgwater, Somerset

Printed in Great Britain

The Orion Publishing Group's policy is to use papers
that are natural, renewable and recyclable products made
from wood grown in sustainable forests. The logging and
manufacturing processes are expected to conform to the
environmental regulations of the country of origin.

www.orionbooks.co.uk

This book is dedicated to my dear friends,
Sophie, William, Madeleine and Josephine Corke,
who lent me their house for the story
and to the memory of W.H. Hudson, who inspired it.

With grateful thanks to Fiona and Jenny.

November 2nd 1798
All Souls

D arkness. Smoke. Weeping.
  A breath of wind parts the smoke and the moon
  appears. A figure stands among burning ruin and
rubble. Beside her, two ghost-faced owls perch on charred
timbers. Smoke envelops them once more.

The weeping ceases.

One

Flight

'They say the south country's creeping with spies.'

Scat Raven wiped the greasy blade of a knife against his sleeve and narrowed his eyes. He scanned the chalk down in the twilight.

His companion, hunched over their fire, prodded the embers with a stick and grunted. Behind their makeshift camp ancient forest gripped the hillside. Before them rose the sheep-cropped turf, scattered with blackthorn and wind crazed trees. Above, the darkening sky was streaked with shreds of lavender and gold.

'Spies for the customs, spies for the filthy French,' Scat

3

muttered. 'Even honest thieving's a danger now.' He picked a sparrow bone from his teeth and spat at the fire. Both men studied the dancing sparks in silence. A fox slipped through the shadows, tainting the dusk with its stench. Among the hills and hollow ways night creatures stirred; bat, badger, smuggler, poacher, runaway, thief.

The second man, Raker, tipped the dregs from his tin cup, stood up and scuffed out the fire with his boot. He picked up a stout club and weighed it in his hand.

'Time for work.'

Scat rummaged among their few belongings.

'Where's the cider pot? I'll carry that last drop where it'll do some good.'

Suddenly the gorse rustled at their back.

Something hit the grass with a thud. Both men swung round. Scat grabbed a staff.

'Who's there?'

They lunged and stabbed at the gorse. A dark shape leapt across a clearing and dived into the nearest scrub. Scat caught a glimpse of a small, pale face.

'It's a lad, stealing our pot.'

'I'll break his head!'

'No, I'll have him, he's mine!'

The figure fled, careering through a thicket, crashing into the undergrowth. At once Scat and Raker thundered after, bellowing curses as they stumbled on anthills and rabbit holes. Flocks of roosting birds took flight. A startled deer bounded into the cover of a spinney beyond. Reaching the open down Scat raised his hand and the two men paused to catch their breath and listen. The fugitive did not lie low for long. They soon saw their quarry further up the hill, silhouetted against the last ribbons of sunset, bent double with a stitch.

'It's a girl!' Raker shook his fist. 'Thievin' witch. I'll take a stick to her.' But Scat held him back. The girl glanced over her shoulder, picked up her skirts and darted off over the hill.

'Let her go, she's not worth the screaming,' said Scat. 'Others will beat a thievin' wench out alone – and worse.' He turned back. 'Anyhow, remember, that was the parson's pot before we emptied his cart and filled it with trussed parson!'

But Raker was in no mood to make light of it. He growled like a dog denied its sport.

'Well, it's dark enough for business now,' said Scat. 'Let's be moving on.'

Megan fled from the two men over the dark downland, towards a track which dropped out of sight among the trees below. Loose nuggets of chalk skittered beneath her feet. She ran from danger. She ran from guilt. From everything she'd ever known . . .

The rutted track sank into a hollow. High banks rose on both sides and leafy branches met above. The only light there seemed to glow from the path itself. Megan's heart thumped so fiercely she thought it would burst. She threw herself at the bank and slammed her fists against the ground. Nettles stung her arms. Megan grasped the stingers and ripped two fistfuls of leaves, grinding her fingers tight into her palms until, with a gasp, she could bear no more. A mash of torn nettle fell from each hand. Her palms swelled with white weals, maggots of throbbing pain. For a moment the pain obliterated everything. All the fear, the panic, drained into those two stinging fires. She took a deep breath, exhausted but too afraid to pause long. Can't stop. Mustn't stop here. I've got to find somewhere to hide. Tugging her skirt from a snatch of brambles she set off at a run once more, down the track to anywhere.

Two

Safe

Megan followed the path as it sloped through the wood until it met a cart track. Which way to go? To the right a glint of water snaked between tall reeds. To the left, a short distance away, candlelight glimmered in a cottage window. For a moment she considered knocking at the cottage door. There would be food there, maybe a kind word. But she was afraid of revealing herself. Turn away, there'll only be questions. Find a safe place to hide and rest. You'll not feel the hunger if you sleep.

Megan stood awhile, unable to draw her eyes from the

tiny golden glow in the darkness. Suddenly a rat scurried across her foot and she stifled a scream. At that very moment, as if her breath had disturbed the flame, the light in the window was extinguished.

Now only a mean rind of moon punctured the darkness. Megan thought of the two men she had seen, out there in the night. What other dangers haunted the black hills and hollow ways? Spies for the customs, spies for the French, fighting men gathering against the invasion ... where was safety? I want to stop running. I want to be still. Slowly, Megan walked towards the silhouette of the house.

As she approached, she found that the house was one of a straggle of cottages at the edge of a village. To her dismay, they were all in ruins, with crumbled walls and tattered thatch. Did I dream the candlelight? she wondered. A dog barked in the distance and she hurried on.

Most of the village was in the same derelict state. A few houses had signs of being inhabited but there was not a flicker of light to suggest anyone stirred within. In the meagre light the whole place had an eerie feeling of misfortune about it. Megan stopped to look over a farmyard gate. The yard was overgrown with weeds and the barns and sheds were neglected. Stable doors hung off their hinges and roofs had lost their tiles. If the farm was empty it might be a good place to hide, she thought. Cautiously Megan pushed the gate open a little and slipped into the moonlit yard. She listened for a whinny or a shuffled hoof, but heard nothing. Like the rest of the village, it seemed mysteriously deserted. Beside the yard was a large house, with chequerboard walls of brick and flint and tall chimneys. Megan guessed it was a manor house. A long thatched wall separated the farmyard from the house. She walked through an archway in the wall and found herself in a kitchen courtyard. All was dark and silent there too. At last, she thought, a safe place.

Megan searched the outbuildings for somewhere to sleep and chose a small cowshed with enough soft hay to make a bed. Hidden in the darkest corner, she bundled her shawl up for a pillow and rested, for the first time in days, without fear.

As she fell into a deep sleep, two white feathers fluttered down beside her.

Megan woke the following morning, feeling hungry. Where am I? she wondered. Lying in the hay, in an abandoned farm, in a desolate village, she was struck by the utter solitude of her situation. It was four days since she'd run away from home, following the ox-droves and the sheep tracks over the Downs, and in all that time she hadn't seen or spoken to a soul. What would they do when they found she had gone? She thought of her parents, locked away in mourning, silent strangers in a dark house. Most likely they would only feel more sorry for themselves. They hated her. They punished her every day for living. Megan felt the injustice flare, hot and fierce inside, burning the fear away. She wanted to cry out: 'It wasn't my fault!' But it was. That was the unbearable part. For so long her parents had rejected her because she wasn't the son they so desperately wanted, until, like a self-fulfilling prophesy, she had truly let them down and destroyed all their hope for the future. She could never go back. But could she ever forget? How far would she have to run to escape the past?

Morning bathed the cowshed with light. A cock crowed. It was a new day. It was *her* new day. Her new life. Megan sniffed back a tear and tugged the hay from her hair, twisting the long brown locks tight and tucking them up beneath her cap. Don't cry, she told herself firmly. You ran away from the crying. You've got to look after yourself now.

She peeped outside. The yard was empty as it had been the night before, so she brushed herself down and crept out in search of some food.

The farm looked as though it had been abandoned long ago. Rakes and scythes lay rusting in the grass, and a cart was so smothered with bindweed it seemed to have grown right out of the earth. As Megan walked among the empty kennels and coops, pigpens and tattered bee skeps, she was disturbed by the absence of beasts and bustle. Maybe there had been some plague here, she thought with a shudder. But there was no sign that the animals had died. Even though it seemed deserted she felt she was trespassing. Her skin prickled and her throat was dry. She didn't believe in ghosts but it wasn't difficult to imagine a pale, hollow-cheeked farm boy rattling his harness in one of those gaping doorways.

Megan decided to investigate the house. Every window she could see was shuttered, except those in the kitchen. She peered inside. A few withered apples lay on the table where a mouse was making a breakfast of them. Megan listened. Not a sound. Nervously she tried the handle. With a flick of his tail the mouse scurried off, but no one appeared. She pushed open the kitchen door and went in. Like the yard, it seemed the house was abandoned. Megan snatched an apple, then pocketed another. She ate hungrily and gazed around; fine dishes and glassware were arranged on high shelves but dirty pots and pipkins were scattered about the room; silver cutlery was strewn on the table, unwashed, a jug lay broken on the flagstone floor and the dusty dresser was draped with cobwebs. It was as if the occupants had left in a hurry, but someone had been here since, disturbing things. There seemed nothing else to eat and the apple had made her thirsty so she went outside to find the well and pulled up a pail. The cool water smelt of moss as she drank from her cupped hands and splashed her face. Feeling a little less apprehensive, now she was sure there was no one about, she waded through a garden of waist-high weeds to the front of the house. Why had such a beautiful house been left uninhabited long enough for thorn bushes to grow around it, like an enchanted fairy-tale castle? There was some story to it and Megan was intrigued. She sat inside the porch and imagined the greetings and partings that must have taken place in that doorway. Now the stone benches were littered with dead leaves and snail shells, and grass grew through the cracked paving.

Megan retraced her steps to the kitchen. It did seem like a perfect place to hide – an empty house all to herself. But there was a haunted feeling about the place that bothered her, about the whole derelict village. She stood in the middle of the room, motionless, listening hard, willing the room to release a whisper of its past – an echo of gossip or grumble, voices raised, secrets shared.

Two storerooms opened off the back of the kitchen; a pantry, containing crocks of oats and flour, lit by a small window, and a buttery, where she found a barrel of salt and bunches of dried herbs that had long since lost their scent and colour. Suddenly she was startled by a crash and swung round. Someone was there! No – a wicker basket rattled across the stone floor, hit the wall and lay, rocking like an empty cradle. She must have brushed it off the shelf with her sleeve. Megan picked it up and sighed, her nerves rattled. What if the occupants of the house should return and find her here? She ran her fingers through the thick dust on the shelf. No one has been in these rooms for a long while, she reassured herself. Still, she *had* seen candlelight in the village last night. It would be best to keep quiet and out of sight. In the pantry a ladder rested against the wall. She climbed up and into an open loft above. The loft ran the whole length and breadth of the kitchen. Half of it was stacked with boxes for storing apples, which still contained a few wrinkled fruit. Beside these was a pile of sacks and a straw mattress with a heap of moth-eaten blankets. A hairbrush with ribbon tied to the handle lay beside it. Perhaps this was where the kitchen maid slept, she thought, imagining the delicious scent of apples up there after harvest, mixed with the cooking smells wafting from the kitchen below. Why had the people of the house vanished? If they had moved or gone away surely things would have been left tidy, or packed up. It was as if some Pied Piper had lured them all away ...

Well, she thought sensibly, picking up the hairbrush, I'll probably never know. What matters is that there's no one around to ask questions. It's a perfect place to take refuge for a while.

Her thoughts were broken by someone whistling for a dog outside in the lane. The familiar sound made her smile it was a touchstone of normality in a strange place. She hurried back down the ladder to look out of the buttery window. But as she reached the last rung Megan sensed a presence in the kitchen behind her.

She froze.

A voice cut the silence.

'Who's there?'

Three

Marguerite

Megan gripped her skirt and slowly turned.

A woman in a faded dress stood in the doorway. A shawl had slipped from her shoulders. White hair, half-pinned, fell haphazardly about her face, which was as pale as parchment. She stared at Megan with hazy eyes.

'Speak. I know you are there.' Her tone was sharp but her voice tremulous, as though she had just been startled from sleep.

Megan stumbled back against the ladder. At once the

woman moved towards her. She held her body rigid, her arms outstretched like a spectre. Megan realised the woman was blind.

'I . . . I thought there was no one here!' she blurted.

'So, it's a girl,' said the woman. 'Forgive me for not hearing you knock at the door.' Her voice softened but Megan thought she could detect a calculating note to it, like the spider greeting the fly.

Megan made up her mind to run. Almost as soon as the thought formed the woman sidestepped, with a swish of her gown, to stand between Megan and the back door. 'Don't be afraid,' she said. Steadying herself by the table she touched an apple core Megan had left there. Her fingertips travelled like insects over the scrap of fruit. 'You must be hungry. An apple's not much of a breakfast.'

'I wasn't thieving,' said Megan. 'I'm not a thief.' She tried to edge towards the other side of the room. But the woman's blank eyes followed her. Deftly she turned and stood, once more between Megan and the door.

'Who are you?' she asked. 'You're not from this village. Why did you come to me?'

'I didn't, I mean I'm not . . .' Megan stuttered. 'I'm passing through.'

'On your own?'

Megan was silent. The woman waited, listening to her hesitation. Reading the silence.

'I'm an orphan,' Megan mumbled at last.

The woman took a sharp breath. At once Megan regretted revealing that she was alone. The woman considered Megan's words for a moment and smiled.

'Then you have come to me.' She swayed and twisted her head from side to side. 'See, my friends, fate has sent us a girl. We *need* a girl.'

What did she mean? Who was she talking to? Megan began to panic. She was trapped.

There was no sound, no sign of anyone else. She's mad, Megan thought. Blind and mad. Megan made a dash for the door but the woman reached it before her.

'Don't be alarmed,' she said, gripping the handle behind her back. 'You find me strange, but it is only my affliction. I live in a dark world, with little company. There has been no one here since my old nurse died.' The woman brushed a lock of hair from her forehead, as if suddenly conscious of her appearance. 'A village girl did come once, but she didn't stay. She stole from us, my friends. She believed her mother's lies. But you have no mother ...'

Megan felt a pain in her chest.

Suddenly the woman fell silent, her head raised as she listened to something.

For several seconds Megan could discern no sound at all, then she heard it, distant at first. The thud of horses' hooves. Someone was riding through the village.

The woman made no move.

Megan's blood pounded in her head. Had someone followed her after all? The woman was looking straight at her.

'Have no fear. No one will find you here,' she said. 'We never open the door to strangers.'

'How do you know it's a stranger?' whispered Megan.

'I know it is not a friend.'

For a moment nothing stirred. Megan and the blind

woman stood together, still as statues. The clatter of hooves grew loud and close then dwindled away down the lane.

'See, you are safe here,' the woman said, more gently now. 'I need someone to help, to cook for me. You could sleep in the apple loft.'

Megan stared at the blind woman. Could she possibly stay with her in this house? She looked around the kitchen. It was far bigger than the one at home. Until Jacob was born she'd spent many hours at Cook's elbow, learning how to bake and stew and roast.

'Take the lid off the crock in the buttery,' instructed the woman. 'The big one by the door.'

Megan did as she was told. She knelt beside the crock and lifted the lid. There, to her astonishment, was a feast of food. Lying on top was a smoked fish wrapped in sorrel leaves. Beneath it was a loaf, some hard pears and a bundle wrapped in muslin. Untying the cloth she found a couple of pasties and a cold, cooked chicken. Megan had eaten nothing but nuts and berries for three days. She breathed in the sweet scents and her stomach gnawed itself with hunger. The woman's offer was tempting. Just to eat a proper meal, just to stop running for a while. She remembered her encounter with the men on the Downs. This was a strange sort of sanctuary but still better than sleeping under a hedge, better, too, than going hungry. And there was nothing to stop her leaving whenever she wished ...

'I can cook a little,' she said hesitantly, rising to her feet.

'Good.' The woman walked slowly but directly towards Megan, until she stood close before her, closer than a person with sight would ever stand, Megan thought. She stiffened. The woman smelt unkempt. She raised her hand to touch Megan's cheek. Megan couldn't stop herself from trembling. She shut her eyes. Slowly the woman traced the contours of Megan's face, her touch as light as a butterfly. Then she put her hands on Megan's shoulders and ran them down her arms, feeling the youthful strength in them. She reached Megan's hands. Her fingers hesitated at the raised wheals, which still smarted there.

'What's this?' she asked.

Megan winced but said nothing. The woman listened, as if hearing things unspoken.

'I fell in nettles,' Megan said at last. 'I tripped, in the dark.' The woman let Megan's hands fall, and took a step back as if Megan's lie had struck her. Whatever she could or couldn't see, thought Megan, nothing was hidden from her.

'Well, they're strong and fit for work,' she said. 'What is your name?'

'Megan.'

'You may call me . . .' The woman hesitated, as if unsure. 'You may call me Marguerite.' This exchange seemed awkward for her. Megan wondered when Marguerite had last received a visitor to this lonely place.

Marguerite pulled her shawl tight around her shoulders. 'Are there the makings of a broth in the crock?' she asked.

Megan thought for a moment. Broth. Cook would stew a poultry carcass with vegetable scraps. 'I could use some chicken,' she replied.

'Very well,' said Marguerite. 'We shall have chicken, my friends. Make it hot, for the cold is in my bones.' Without further instruction she turned and walked away into the dark interior of the house.

Megan waited until she heard Marguerite's footsteps fade away before she raced back to the buttery and tore a crust off the golden loaf. For a moment, sitting there on the dirty floor in the blind woman's house, she cared about nothing else in the world.

Later, Megan sat back to consider her situation. This may be my first good fortune, she thought. I won't be found here. I can take time to decide what to do next. She remembered the paper boats she used to make for her brother Jacob to sail on the river at the bottom of the garden; how they would lie together on the jetty and set a boat on the water, pushing it through the reeds until it lurched free and rocked away out of sight; how they would imagine its voyage ahead, making up tales fraught with danger and adventure.

Now, like the little boats, she was free, adrift in the world – only she'd never looked ahead to what might happen next. One thing she was sure of, she would never return. That life is over, she thought. I'm going to be myself now.

But what did that mean? Megan didn't know any more.

Long ago, after the first babies died, she had learnt not to ask questions, not to complain, not to cry. She'd kept her thoughts and feelings inside, in her own private world, until they became so painful that she'd learnt to silence them there too.

Then Jacob came. He was a miracle, her parents said. For a short while all the unhappiness was forgotten, they were so giddy with the joyful rush of living after many long years of grief. Jacob made sense of everything. They were a family. With him, Megan could talk, laugh, sing and cry.

Now it was strange – she could hardly remember what that time felt like. When Jacob died she'd hidden away again; beyond candlelight, behind curtains, curled up in the linen cupboard, lonely, listening, unseen. Only Cook had ever noticed, taking her hand and bringing her to the warmth and brightness of the kitchen. 'You must step out of the shadows, child,' she said. 'There's only pain in the dark corners of this house. Look the world in the eye, Meg, and believe in yourself.'

Now Megan stared through the blind woman's kitchen into the dark shuttered house beyond. It seemed she had stepped out of the shadows of one gloomy place and into another. No one would take her hand here. Like the little paper boats on the river, she had no map or compass. I have to learn to be strong for myself and look the world in the eye, she thought. That will be my journey …

But just now she was too tired to move on again. She wondered what Marguerite would ask of her. Would it be only to cook? Why else did she need a girl? The blind woman made her nervous; that crazed stare, the twitching hands quivering like creatures with a life of their own, the iron will in her quiet voice. Megan shuddered. And what about the friends she spoke to – were they phantoms of her mind?

I'll stay two days, no more, she decided. I'll get my strength back, make a plan then I'll move on. Somebody must have brought food to fill the crock. Maybe they could help me.

Megan set about making the chicken broth. The fireplace was thick with ash, so first she swept it out, then she found the woodshed and brought in an armful of logs and kindling. But how to light it? Megan had watched the maid use a strike-a-light at home. She hunted all over the kitchen until she found a small pouch containing a flattened iron ring, a wedge of flint and a handful of dry moss. Megan laid the fire and placed the moss on the hearthstone beside it. Then she struck the iron with the flint and tried to catch a spark in the moss. It was much harder than she'd imagined, but eventually her persistence was rewarded. She tucked the burning moss between the sticks and they caught alight. Before long Megan had a crackling fire burning in the grate. She smiled to herself. Life was kindled in the cold heart of the house.

While the fire built up a cooking heat Megan fetched water and scrubbed the table. Outside the morning sun was already hot. She took a rag to the grimy kitchen windows to let the sunlight in. After days of running in fear, it felt good to be busy at a simple task. As she worked she thought about the blind woman living alone there. The food in the crock could be eaten cold, but how did she manage without a fire in winter? How did she heat water to bathe or wash clothes? Who came when she was ill? Megan couldn't imagine how anyone with such an affliction lived without help. She could see that Marguerite might frighten people away; there was something tormented in her manner, something haunted about her gaunt face.

When the broth was bubbling and the smell penetrated the rest of the house Marguerite appeared in the doorway once more.

'Bring the food into the parlour,' she said, startling Megan, who had not heard her approach.

Megan spooned out a bowl of the steaming, savoury soup and followed Marguerite out of the kitchen into a dark hallway. The parlour was directly beyond the kitchen. Apart from splinters of light coming through the broken shutters, the room was dark. A long table, with cobwebbed candlesticks and empty platters, occupied the centre of the room. In the gloom Megan could make out wall hangings and curtains. The chairs and a fire screen were disarranged, as if they had been moved out of the way and never put back where they belonged. There was a big hearth, messy with ash, and a pair of bellows lying in it. A few logs were stacked untidily in the inglenook. No fire had burned there for a long time.

Marguerite sat at the table, straight-backed and still, at ease in the darkness.

'I'll need to know where things are, for the table, that is,' Megan ventured shyly.

Marguerite nodded towards a cupboard where Megan found what she needed. Nervously she laid the table and placed the chicken broth before Marguerite. To her surprise, Marguerite picked up the bowl and supped the hot soup straight from it, without reaching for a spoon. Megan was relieved to see that it pleased her.

As the cuffs of Marguerite's sleeves slipped back Megan noticed her thin wrists. No wonder she's so cold, thought Megan, for although the day was warm, the sunless room was chill and damp.

'Shall I light the in fire here?' she suggested.

'Fire!' Marguerite raised her head. 'No fire, not here,' she said abruptly. Muttering something else Megan couldn't understand, she waved her away and lifted the broth to her lips once more.

Megan took her own food out into the yard and sat on the grass in the shade of the chicken house. There she soaked up the broth with a crust of bread and enjoyed a chicken leg as if it were a king's feast.

A robin hopped down from the wall and settled on an upturned bucket nearby. It sang a trill of insistent notes as if calling Megan's attention. At once it reminded her of another robin – a bird which had flown through the window and perched on the bedpost when one of the babies died. She remembered standing in the rain later that day, watching the undertaker carry the little coffin out to his cart.

'A boy?' he had asked her father, pausing beside him in the road.

'Third in five years,' her father answered, putting a bag of coins into the undertaker's pocket. As she watched the small, weightless coffin laid in the cart, the robin flew up again and settled on the box.

When she thought about it, there had always been a bird. Moments after the first baby died a blackbird had walked right in at the door. The second time a thrush sang, although it was deepest night. 'They come for the little soul,' her mother had told her. 'To take it up to the Everafter.'

As the undertaker's horse pulled away, Megan had watched the robin fly above the cart, then dart away into the grey rain. 'Poor tiny baby,' she whispered. 'See, the sky is crying for you.' He hadn't even lived long enough to have a name. But he was her brother, just the same. Tears streamed down her cheeks. She turned to her father who was walking back to the house.

'Father!' she cried, running to catch up with him. But he didn't turn around.

Megan was roused from her memories by a bell ringing inside. The robin was gone. Wiping her fingers on her skirt she went back inside the house.

The parlour door was open and the room empty. Megan cleared the dishes in the dim light and closed the door behind her.

She returned to her self-appointed task of making order

in the kitchen. The effort distracted her from thoughts of home, of what she'd done, of what to do next. All afternoon she cleaned, scrubbing the flagstone floor until her fingers were raw from wringing out the cloth. And yet she couldn't shake the feeling that she was being watched. Every now and then she spun round, certain she would see Marguerite in the doorway. But there was never anyone there.

As twilight descended Megan searched for candles but couldn't find any. Wearily, she climbed the ladder to the apple loft and sank onto the mattress. She shut her eyes and bathed in the day's heat still radiating from the sloping roof above. All was quiet except for the rustle of the straw stuffing beneath her body. She was exhausted from her day's work, yet sleep wouldn't come. Her mind wandered through memories; a narrow wooden box on the floor, a child curled beneath the blankets of her bed, a musty black dress and bonnet; her parents turning away in the shadows, low voices muttering her name, accusations, words of shame. Guilt stalked every one. She could run away from her home but how could she ever run away from her past?

Too tired to think or feel any more, Megan unlaced her woollen overskirt and rolled it up for a pillow then, at last, she fell into a restless sleep.

Bats flitted in the roof space and outside a vixen called to her mate. The thatch crackled as it cooled in the night air. Then – tap, tap, tap – Megan heard a brittle, insistent sound, somewhere close. After a while the tapping paused, as if someone or something was listening for an answer. It started again. Coming to a little, Megan noticed a window set in the roof. She stared, sleepy and confused. Something was tapping on the glass. Through the filthy pane she could make out an indistinct shape – the face of a child. Megan crawled to the window and tried to free the stiff latch. It took a wrench to force it open. There, in the darkness was a small boy with white, moonlit wings.

She froze. For a brief moment the boy stared at her with tear-stained eyes. He whimpered, as though he'd lost all hope of comfort, and then turned away and flew towards the church tower. Megan thrust her head and shoulders out into the starry night and flung her arms after him, crying out, 'Come back!' but her voice made no sound and the darkness swallowed him. A deathly chill gripped her. At last, numb and shivering, Megan roused herself, rubbed her eyes and closed the window, forcing the latch shut. But as she turned back to her bed she saw him. Lying, lifeless, on the dusty floor. His wings broken.

Four

Haunted

Megan woke before dawn, but the dream stayed with her.

She lay in the darkness and saw her brother's face. Jacob, the boy who lived. The miracle her mother had given up praying for.

Megan's memories of him were her treasures. So small and frail at first, Megan remembered the wonder of his tiny hand curled around her finger. The new skin almost too soft to touch. The sweet smell of his muslin, which she would hold to her cheek when he was asleep. Doted on by all, he grew into a strong, happy child and at last the house echoed with laughter, with rhymes and games and mischief.

But why? thought Megan. Why wasn't that enough for him?

As Jacob grew strong, his spirit grew wild and free. Not content to sit with his playthings, he loved to roam the meadows chasing butterflies, or watch swallows skim the river at the bottom of the garden. Most of all he loved to watch their father's falcon fly. From the moment he first saw it Jacob could talk of nothing else and he began to dream of flying himself. In his dreams he soared beyond the garden, beyond the river, beyond the water meadows to imaginary skies. 'And all the birds follow,' he used to tell Megan, wide-eyed, 'all the butterflies and dragonflies and every tiny thing with wings, all following, fluttering over the clouds.

Sometimes he would wake sobbing that his dreams were not reality. 'I know I can do it, Meggie. I know what it feels like – you just think yourself into the sky and spread your arms and ... and it just has to be true.'

Then Megan would comfort him and secretly wish she could dream it too. Now she wished she had distracted him from this yearning to fly. If only she'd persuaded him to be content.

Her foreboding began when Jacob started to run down the sloping lawn, gathering speed, breathless, flapping his arms like wings.

'Look at me, Meggie,' he would call to her. 'See, I am a bird. I can fly!' At the bottom of the lawn he would swoop and swerve, then race to the top again, his bright eyes full of sky.

Megan watched over Jacob. Each day she warned him not

to run as far as the little jetty that stood out over the water. The river there was deep and thick with weeds. 'You'll drown for sure if you fall in,' she told him. But with the wind in his hair and his arms flung wide Jacob had no care. 'Then I'll be an angel,' he laughed, 'and have real wings and I'll fly like an angel-bird high above you all day long!'

'Don't say that!' she had cried. 'Don't even think it!' But he only ran faster, whooping with joy, spinning and soaring until he fell dizzy at her feet.

Jacob had run and skipped through their lives so briefly it seemed now to Megan that he had always been on his way to somewhere else. Just staying with them a while, like the swallows in summer. But he belonged to them. She should have saved him ... now it was too late. 'Why must you haunt me?' she whispered into the darkness. 'Why won't you let me go? Leave me, Jacob. Give me peace. You have your dream now, you can fly free.'

Again she remembered the boy in her dream, lying broken beneath his wings.

What had she done?

Five

Morne

Megan awoke from an uneasy sleep to the first
light glowing softly through the buttery window
below. She wrapped a blanket around her
shoulders and stumbled down the ladder, yawning. To her
surprise a loaf and some eggs had been left on the kitchen
table and beside them lay a bundle of rush candles. She
fingered the soft wax, puzzling why anyone would bring
candles for a blind woman. Unless . . . could they have been
left for me? Whoever brought them must know I'm here.
A shiver ran through her. Had someone been watching her?
Were they watching now? Megan opened the kitchen door

but the house was wrapped in morning mist and the mysterious visitor nowhere to be seen. A thousand spider webs hung around the yard, beaded with dew, delicately arranged to trap their morning prey. All was silent and still. I should be grateful, Megan thought as she pulled the blanket tight against the damp air. After all, the candles are a kindness. But she could not dispel the uncomfortable feeling that someone was watching the house.

Megan stoked the fire and helped herself to some bread. Afraid of being surprised again by Marguerite, she made sure not to turn her back to the door and listened all the while for a creaking stair or the swish of a gown. But Marguerite did not appear.

By the time she had finished eating the mist had dissolved in the morning sun. It would be another hot day. Megan decided to explore outside. This time she turned to the back of the kitchen, where she found herself in a small courtyard. Something white lying between the flint cobbles caught her eye. Megan picked it up. It was a broken clay pipe. She turned the sooty stem in her hand, wondering about the last person to hold it. Someone must have smoked that pipe here in the days when the house bustled with life, sitting on the bench listening to farm boys shout and scullery maids clattering dishes in the kitchen. What would he think of that empty, silent place now? The little fragment of pipe filled her with melancholy. Things you expected to last forever – life in that house, the farm, the babies who'd hardly begun to live, Jacob. All lost. Why could nothing be trusted to last?

Suddenly Megan sensed eyes upon her. She dropped the pipe and swung around ... but the doorway was empty, all the window shutters closed. Nothing in the garden stirred. Yet she *knew* she was being watched, as sure as if someone had put a hand upon her shoulder. She ran towards the yard but, before she reached it, the click of a latch stopped her dead. Megan's heart pounded. She couldn't tell if the sound had come from the farm gate or the kitchen door. Was she being watched from outside or in? She made a dash for the house, for the refuge of the loft.

But as soon as Megan reached the first rung of the ladder the bell rang. She stepped down and took a deep breath. Calm. It was your imagination. A noise elsewhere. A blind woman couldn't move about the house so quickly. And, after all, how could she watch when she cannot see ...

When Megan entered the parlour she found Marguerite sitting calmly at the table. There was no hint of fluster about her. Her hair was scraped into a skewed chignon and she wore the same sprigged muslin morning dress she had worn the day before. Megan noticed now that the dress was of a style long out of fashion, stained and badly crumpled, as if it had been slept in. Despite this she appeared to Megan like some tragic queen, imperious and proud, though her castle was only inhabited by ghosts.

'So, you have walked in my garden,' said Marguerite.

Megan started. She had been watching after all!

'Can you see a little?' she asked awkwardly.

'I see nothing.' Marguerite raised her hands to her eyes and rubbed her brows as if she might draw the blindness away. 'But I know everything. Others watch for me.'

She *is* mad, thought Megan, staring in horror. 'I thought you lived alone,' she said.

'Alone, yes. Always alone.' Marguerite was silent for a moment. Then she looked up, bewildered, as if waking from sleep. 'Is there milk?' she asked.

'Someone left candles and a loaf,' Megan replied, 'but I haven't seen any milk.'

'Then you must fetch it. Take a pitcher to Tawks Farm, at East End. The farmer's wife will see to it.'

'How shall I pay?' asked Megan.

Marguerite looked surprised. 'Pay? I have told you, the farmer's wife will see to it. We have an arrangement.' She ran her fingers along the row of pearl buttons on her cuff, like a nun with rosary beads, and muttered faintly, 'When she returns we shall have milk pudding, my friends.' Then she turned to Megan. 'Ring the bell when you are done.'

'How will I find Tawks Farm?' asked Megan.

Marguerite pointed to the window. 'You have eyes to read shadows. East End, I said. It's the only farm now. Gulls have been following the plough all morning, haven't you heard?'

Megan was troubled by Marguerite's changeable mood and imaginary companions. There was no sign of others in the house. Not living, anyway. Maybe they were visions, or ghosts ...

She fetched a pitcher and stepped out of the gate. No one was about, not a child playing in the lane or even a dog idling along the path. Only the rattle of a grasshopper pricked the empty silence.

Megan studied the village. The single lane stretched left and right as far as she could see. In daylight the true state of the cottages was revealed to Megan – ragged thatches shed their straw, plaster crumbled and ivy gripped the brickwork. Only half a dozen scattered among them had smoke curling from their chimneys and their gardens tended.

Opposite the Manor, Megan saw a deserted smithy. She crossed the lane to take a look and peered through a chink in the door. In the faint light she could just make out shadowy heaps of ironwork lying beside the cold furnace, the huge, impotent bellows and the blacksmith's leather apron hanging from a peg on the wall. No blazing fire belching sparks and smoke; no hammer strike ringing the anvil; no bending and breaking, no mending and making. As if the blacksmith had simply laid down his tools and walked away.

It was nearing midday. Megan eyed the stump of her shadow and turned east along the lane. She passed more empty cottages until she came to a neat garden of vegetables growing outside a small, whitewashed house. A caged canary hung beside the door, warbling in a splash of sunlight. As Megan stopped to watch the yellow bird hop hopelessly from side to side something stirred in the shadow of the porch. An old man in a shepherd's smock sat on a bench puffing smoke rings from his pipe.

'Good morning,' she said shyly.

The old man said nothing. He drew on his pipe and studied her. After a moment he nodded at the pitcher Megan was carrying.

'You must have walked a fair way to fill that crock, being a stranger here,' he said, eyeing her with curiosity.

'I'm after milk from Tawks Farm,' Megan replied.

'Who for?'

'For the big house.'

'Who d'ye say?'

Megan spoke a little louder. 'For Marguerite.'

At the sound of her name the old man scowled hard. 'She'll sour it, see if she don't, mark my words!' He muttered something under his breath and waved dismissively towards the Manor, shaking his head. Without another word he stabbed his stick into the ground, rose to his feet and hobbled inside.

Megan was taken aback by the old man's unfriendliness. She continued through the village. Twice she glimpsed a face at a window. Further along she heard someone chopping firewood, but not one horse or cart passed her on the road, there were no women leaning over their gates to chat in the sun. Megan wondered what sort of reception she would find at Tawks Farm ...

The lane divided and she took the eastward track that bridged a dry ditch and rose gently among ash trees towards a large farmhouse.

Contrary to what Megan had expected, Tawks Farm was evidently thriving, bustling with chickens and geese. Well-thatched hayricks towered in the rickyard, pigs grunted, two mares peered nosily from their stables and freshly washed linen lay on the hedge to bleach. This was a happier place, thought Megan. Whatever gloom seemed to infect the rest of the village hadn't reached here. She knocked at the kitchen door. A baby cried and voices called to each other inside. After a moment a stout, silver-haired woman appeared, wearing an apron stained with berry juice.

'And who are you, now?' said the woman, pinning back a stray curl. She leant against the doorframe and smiled at Megan.

There was something about the woman's strong, fair face that Megan trusted at once. She gave her name.

'You're not from the village?' The woman reached across to a table inside the door and brought out a couple of plums. She handed one to Megan who ate the golden fruit gratefully.

'I'm just passing through,' said Megan, as she slipped the stone from her lips. 'What is this village – what is it called?'

'Morne,' said the woman. She cast her stone into the garden. 'You must have come far if you've not heard talk of it.'

'What is the talk?' asked Megan, puzzled by what she meant.

The woman pushed her sleeves up her brown arms. 'Just gossip, as ever was,' she said.

Megan held out the pitcher. 'I've come for milk, for Marguerite.'

The woman stiffened. 'You're Marguerite's help?' Her genial mood disappeared. Businesslike, she took the pitcher from Megan and strode past her to the dairy across the yard, scattering chickens in her path. Megan followed.

'She doesn't usually ask for milk,' the woman said.

'She wants me to make a pudding,' said Megan.

'Pudding indeed!' The woman filled the pitcher with milk and handed it back to Megan.

'You'll not find many friends in this village, Megan,' she said as she wiped her hands on her apron. Megan heard the warning in her voice. 'It's nothing of your doing, but don't expect much from folk while you're at the Manor.' She turned away and started back to the kitchen. 'There's always milk here,' she called over her shoulder. 'And my Jack takes a basket of food most days and fills the crock, like he promised her. Leave him a note for what you want, but don't expect much from anyone else.' And with that she shut the kitchen door firmly behind her.

Megan made her way back down the lane, clutching the heavy pitcher, astonished by the change in the farmer's wife and the old man at the mention of Marguerite's name. What could the blind woman have done to be regarded so coldly? She was intrigued to know more.

Suddenly Megan became aware she wasn't alone. Without turning she quickened her pace over the bridge and followed the lane into the village. Still she felt eyes upon her. A presence, close and intense. She gripped the pitcher, trying not to spill the milk, and walked faster, tugging her skirt up to stop it wrapping around her legs. Maybe I should slow down and let them pass, Megan thought. I have no one to fear here. Yet she sensed menace at her back, closing upon her. Taking a deep breath she slowed her step and lowered her eyes. But whoever followed didn't pass. At last Megan could bear it no longer, she gathered her courage and turned to look over her shoulder. Two barn owls flew close behind her, side by side, low and slow. Their broad white wings beat silently together, flexed talons hung below. Two pairs of black, unblinking eyes met hers. Megan screamed. She stumbled on a flint in the path, milk spilled down her skirt and the wet pitcher almost slipped from her arms.

'Get away,' she cried, waving one arm awkwardly in the air. But the birds buried their ghost-like heads deeper into their chests as if truly intent on pursuing her. Megan panicked. She ran along the path as fast as she could, splattering herself with milk, kicking up the chalk dust in her fear of beak and claw. Just as she reached the Manor House Megan felt the wind of their wings. She flinched. The birds flew over her head, swooped into the yard before her and up to an open attic window. There they came to rest on the ledge, then disappeared, one by one, into the darkness beyond.

As Megan watched a hand closed the window behind them.

Six

Night and Day

All afternoon Megan kept watch at the kitchen window for a glimpse of the two owls but she didn't see them leave the house. When she had cooked the pudding, with what was left of the milk, she carried it nervously through to the parlour, rang the bell and slipped back to the kitchen. But Marguerite did not come downstairs. The food was left uneaten.

Megan retreated to the loft and sat listening for the owls, close by in the house somewhere. With a finger, she traced the crescent scar above her lip. Ever since her father's falcon had taken fright and lashed out at her she'd been terrified of predatory birds. Now, when she closed her eyes all she saw were those moon-like faces; their eyes black with malice. The owls at her back, the birds that appeared when the babies died, Jacob's winged figure in her dream ...

A stinging sensation made Megan realise she'd been absently scratching at her palms. Cupping her sore hands to her lips she linked thumbs and stretched her fingers wide. 'Go 'way birds,' she whispered, 'go 'way. Be gone!' She willed them all to fly from her mind. As if in answer, a piercing shriek ripped through the air. Megan leapt to her feet, trembling uncontrollably. They were here, somewhere nearby. At once she saw the talons, the hunter's eyes. They'd come for her. Grabbing her shawl she clambered down the ladder, losing her footing on the last rung. She flung open the kitchen door and rushed out into the dusk.

At the yard gate Megan stopped. She rubbed hot tears from her cheeks. Where should she go? Before her stretched the lane, the village, the Downs, the whole world. The thought of setting off alone once more into the night, into the hunting hours, filled her with terror.

She held her breath, listening for beating wings, watching for a flit of white against the black trees, turning wide-eyed to the bat-stirred shadows at her back. But nothing appeared, except a moth dancing crookedly for a moment above her head. She wrapped her arms around herself, rocking calm against the gate. Unwilling to stay yet too afraid to go, at last she turned reluctantly back to the house.

Megan's fitful sleep was broken in the middle of the night by the bell. Drowsy and confused, it took her a moment to wake up. The bell rang again, more urgently now. She pulled on her clothes and stumbled down to the kitchen. Outside, the moon was nothing more than a scatter of pale flecks among the trees. Megan lit a candle and made her way to the parlour.

Marguerite was sitting at the table, fully dressed, the milk pudding dish empty before her.

'Is there more?' she asked, as Megan entered the room. Catching the scent of the candle, she looked surprised. 'What, is it night?'

'Yes,' said Megan, unable to stifle a yawn. 'Deep into it.' She put the candle on the table between them.

Marguerite held the palm of her hand to the heat of the flame. It illuminated her fingers and face. For a moment her skin looked radiant and soft, so different from its daylight pallor. Megan could just make out Marguerite's eyes behind the milky film that obscured them.

'Night and day,' said Marguerite. 'They are the same to me.'

'Was it always so?' asked Megan.

Marguerite withdrew her hand. 'No,' she said, the light gone from her face. 'It is my punishment.'

Megan was shocked and suddenly ashamed of her prying. To be punished by blindness sounded like a judgement from the bible her father used to read aloud on Sundays. Despite Marguerite's severe manner, Megan felt for her.

'I'm sorry,' she said quietly.

Marguerite fussed with her high lace collar. 'We suffer the fate we deserve, there's no more to be said.' She tapped the collar button at her throat, as if to be sure that it secured her pain safely inside.

'But what about you, child? Why has fate abandoned you here?'

Megan shifted uncomfortably. Her weary head had started to throb. I have no answer to that myself, she thought.

Marguerite reached out to touch Megan's face. Megan wanted to draw back but she let the cold fingertips read the contours of her brow.

'I don't believe you are an orphan,' said Marguerite thoughtfully. 'I think you have run away.'

Megan tensed and knew, in an instant, she'd given herself away.

Marguerite rested her hands in her lap. 'What did you run from?' she said. 'Tell me your story, Megan. Secrets give us no peace.'

No one had ever asked Megan to speak about herself before. With surprise she realised how desperately she wanted to tell. Marguerite was right – secrets had given her no peace. But she was too afraid to speak. Afraid of Marguerite. Afraid to let loose the hurt and guilt bound so tight inside her, so tight, so heavy, it lay like a stone in her heart.

The lie came easily. 'I am an orphan,' she said. 'I have no family. No parents.' After all, it was barely a lie at all.

Marguerite frowned but said nothing. With a sigh she rose from her chair. As she passed Megan she paused to stroke her hair and Megan suddenly wanted to cry. Then the blind woman left the room, passing into darkness as if walking in the midday sun.

Seven

Curiosity

Next morning Megan went out, determined to discover the window where the owls had entered the house. She found it, high up between the eaves of the roof. The ledge and the wall below were fouled with birdlime. One of the four shutters was pushed open. At the sound of her footstep in the yard the curtains inside stirred and a white bird sidled onto the sill. Its mask-like face turned towards her, unblinking. If Megan hadn't seen it move she might have taken it for a stuffed bird. As she stood, transfixed, the bird slowly rotated its head until it looked back over its shoulder, then, twisting its body to follow, hopped from one foot to the other and disappeared into the room.

So, it was true – the owls lived there, in the garret. Perhaps they were the companions Marguerite talked to. The thought of meeting them in the dark house filled Megan with dread. She imagined the state of the garret room, filthy with feathers and pellets, reeking like the falcon's cage had done once her father stopped flying the bird. The parlour bell rang and Megan suddenly felt anxious at having to go back inside. I could just walk away, out of the village, she thought. There's no locked gate, I've no belongings to fetch. She tore a rosehip from its stem and crushed its plump belly between her palms, letting the blood red fragments fall from her fingers. Although she was afraid of the birds something compelled her to stay. It was a strange, gloomy house of secrets and yet she felt there was a place for her here. A safe place to hide. Darkness and silence had always been her sanctuary. And despite Marguerite's unnerving manner there was a mystery about her that fascinated Megan. Marguerite needed help, she thought. Maybe the birds would keep away.

The bell rang again, louder this time. Megan rubbed her hands on her apron, turned on her heel and made her way back to the kitchen.

Megan wanted to talk to Marguerite about the birds. But when she brought dinner to the parlour she didn't have the

45

courage to ask. Whatever relationship Marguerite had with the two owls Megan sensed there was something unnatural and oppressive about it. Instead she asked about Tawks Farm and the arrangement for delivering food.

'We have an understanding,' explained Marguerite. 'I gave Jack Sharpe land, long ago, the best farmland in the village. In exchange he brings me what supplies I need, food and wood for the fire.'

'His wife was kind,' said Megan.

'Kind? They do me no kindness,' said Marguerite haughtily. 'We have a contract, that's all. They honour it.'

So that's what happened to the farm, thought Megan. She had to bargain for help. Again, she felt Marguerite's defiant loneliness.

Megan pulled the parlour door shut behind her and glanced towards the staircase in the hall. Although the whole house was shuttered, a column of light fell through the stairwell, from a window somewhere above. As she gazed up a white feather floated down, spiralling slowly until it tumbled off the bottom stair and slipped across the tiles, landing at her feet. She picked it up and held the feather to the light. It was so delicate, so pure. A whiteness so intense it might have fallen from an angel's wing. Megan could not resist the draw of the birds in the house. Repulsed yet fascinated, she had to know more. She stepped on the first stair, which creaked as it took her weight. From the parlour came the clink of a dish disturbed on the table. Megan froze and held her breath, but Marguerite did not appear. She continued, testing each stair cautiously, taking care to walk up the edge of the broad treads so as not to make a noise. The staircase turned at the first floor, opening into a narrow passage, which ran left and right with a room at each end. Megan noticed a rank, musty smell. Another feather was caught in the ornate frame of a mirror. On the windowsill lay a pellet of hair, fur and bone. The birds were in the house, then, and not just in the garret. She approached the right hand door slowly and listened. No sound. As she gripped the handle her foot touched something sharp and smooth. Megan picked the object up in her apron and took it to the stairwell. There, in her hand, was a rat's skull; picked clean, its teeth bared. She threw it to the floor in disgust. Suddenly she lost her nerve and swung back to the stairs. Halfway down she slipped and fell, right at Marguerite's feet.

'So, you would steal from me, Megan.' Marguerite reached out, grabbed Megan's wrist and pulled her to her feet with surprising strength.

'I wasn't stealing,' gasped Megan as Marguerite released her hand. 'I ... I was after linen for my bed.'

Marguerite considered Megan's explanation for a moment. 'Why didn't you ask?' she said at last. 'Everything you need is here.' She pulled a ring of keys from her pocket. 'Come, I will show you.' She started up the stairs.

'There was something else,' said Megan, rubbing her bruised shoulder and steadying her nerves. 'Something I do want to ask ...'

Marguerite stopped but didn't turn.

'The birds,' said Megan. 'Two owls. I saw them fly in at the window yesterday. Do they, are they . . . ?' she stuttered and fell silent.

Marguerite turned slowly. Her dark silhouette towered over Megan. 'You saw my friends, yes,' she murmured. 'They are my eyes.'

'I don't understand,' said Megan.

'How else could I see?' replied Marguerite. 'They watch for me. Nothing is hidden from them. They see all that happens in Morne and all that happens here, in every corner of this house.' Megan felt sick in her stomach. The terrifying thought of the blind woman seeing through the eyes of these owls; of the birds at her bidding, made Megan's body started to shake, as if she'd been plunged into icy water.

'I hear your fear, but the birds will not harm you.' Marguerite clutched the banister and stepped down a stair towards Megan, letting the shawl fall from her shoulders. Megan stumbled backwards, but Marguerite followed the rustle of Megan's skirt with her blind eyes. She stretched out her arms, her long white fingers quivering as if she was drawing in the darkness around them. 'Do not be afraid. We need each other, you and I. Fate has brought you to me.' She stepped closer and the stair cracked like gunshot. 'I have waited so long. I know that you are hiding from something and I have the world hidden from me. But, you see, we can help each other. You have nothing and I have no one.' She took another step towards Megan. 'Do not think to leave me now. My friends will watch you, by night and day. They are no common creatures. They will tell me your thoughts, your secrets. They will even listen to your dreams . . .'

48

Megan turned and ran away – out of the house, out of the yard, once more along the lane to anywhere.

A woman throwing a bucket of slop water into the ditch straightened to watch as Megan fled through the village. She pounded past the path to the church, past a pair of goats tethered on the green, past cottages huddled along the west lane, on and on until she was short of breath, until she'd left all trace of humankind behind and reached a crossways on a broad, empty road. Left, right and beyond, the dusty track disappeared over the Downs, to somewhere else unseen, unknown. Megan threw herself down on the grass, panting and crying. She thumped her fists on the thin soil, drumming them into the chalk.

'What have I done? What will become of me?' A mockery of rooks answered with cruel caws. She buried her head in her throbbing hands. The owls flew up and perched on a thorn tree beside her. With a shriek the rooks took flight.

Maybe Marguerite is right, she thought miserably as her tears subsided. Fate *has* brought me here. Maybe I *am* like her, I'll never escape my punishment.

Jacob, Jacob, I'm sorry. I didn't know what to do. And now I can't make it right. If only she could hold his wet, limp body in her arms again, hold him so close that her own life would pulse into his veins ...

But it was impossible. Everything was impossible. She felt trapped, paralysed, unable to act or think.

Raising her head, Megan saw the owls. For a moment she was too wretched even to be afraid. She sat up, brushed the wet hair from her eyes and studied their white, heart-shaped faces. Each was framed with a narrow ruffle of golden feathers. They tipped their heads in unison as if acknowledging her gaze, their glassy button eyes black as elderberries and the soft white down around them bled with rust. One scratched at its beak with a claw. The other began to preen its wing. She noticed their breasts were specked with smuts as if they'd ventured too close to a fire, their stubby beaks sharp, and talons hooked like pincers. Both stopped and stared intently at her, inscrutable as a pair of judges. She wondered how far they would follow her, but she knew there was no escape from what really haunted her. So she sat at the crossways, unable to go back but unable to go on, heavy with the stone of guilt in her heart, beneath the gaze of Marguerite's owl eyes.

At last, dusk began to fall. Megan's head ached. The fear had drained out of her. She saw now that the birds intended to do her no physical harm. But their stare was so intense she almost believed they heard her thoughts, guessed her secrets.

They knew, and she knew, that there was really only one place to go. She rose wearily and turned back towards the village. As she trudged along the lane something Marguerite had said echoed in Megan's mind. 'We can help each other.' Like Marguerite's hand fleetingly stroking her hair, there was unexpected comfort in it. Despite the owls, despite Marguerite's threats, Megan found she wanted to believe it. To help, to be helped. After all, she thought, watching the first stars prick the darkening sky, Marguerite must be just as lonely as I am.

When Megan returned to the Manor House that evening she found a pile of folded linen and a pillow on the table.

Eight

Fear

Megan decided to stay at the Manor and keep away from the birds as much as possible. When Marguerite came to the parlour next morning she made no reference to their exchange the day before and seemed pleased that Megan had returned, giving her the key to the little room above the porch where the linen was kept. If the owls were in the house they were nowhere to be seen and, to Megan's relief, she saw them fly off into the trees that evening.

The following day Marguerite came into the kitchen carrying a dove-grey skirt, embroidered with crewelwork.

Megan cleared the table and laid it out admiringly.

'You may wear it,' said Marguerite. 'I am too tall and it will keep you warm.' Megan was grateful, for although the late summer sun still blazed outside, inside the house it was cold as winter. Megan traced the fine silk stitching around the hem of the skirt. She held it against her and the length was just right.

'Thank you,' she said shyly. 'I've never been given such a gift. It's the most beautiful skirt I've ever seen.'

Marguerite smiled. 'Would you like to see more?' she asked.

Megan hesitated, afraid to go into Marguerite's room for fear of meeting the birds.

'They were my mother's,' said Marguerite, as if she'd guessed Megan's thoughts. 'She came from wealthy people, brought up with the most exquisite taste. There are gowns trimmed with French lace and ribbons sent from London.'

Megan followed Marguerite upstairs to the first floor. She opened the door to a room as dark as the parlour below but scented with the heavy musk of old perfume.

'Shall I open the shutters?' suggested Megan, but Marguerite would have nothing disturbed, so instead she fetched a candle. As light bloomed in the room it sparkled and glistened like a treasure cave. Megan was astonished. She had never seen such adornments before. Jewellery hung on gilt-framed mirrors, bottles of coloured glass, ointment jars and a pearl-backed brush lay on a dressing table. Chintz covered chairs were draped with silk stockings and satin shawls. Marguerite sat on the bed.

'Look in the dressing room.' She pointed to another door. Megan did as she was told and stared, wide-eyed, at the gowns hanging there. 'It's like a fairy-tale!' she gasped.

'That's just what I used to think when I was a girl,' said Marguerite. 'Bring one to me, bring me the primrose silk.' Megan fingered the fine dresses. They rustled and breathed their perfumes as they swayed. She found the yellow silk and brought it to Marguerite who held it to her cheek. 'This was my favourite,' she murmured. 'This one she always wore on Easter day, when all the village children would come for egg-tapping in the garden. When the light caught it she seemed to shine like a sun. See here,' she fumbled with the skirt until she found a tiny tear, 'this is where she tore it on a bramble, going after a boy who dropped his basket and cried.'

'It would be easy to mend.' Megan studied the broken threads.

'She never noticed the tear,' said Marguerite softly, 'and she never lived to wear it again.'

'I'm sorry.' Megan wondered how often the blind woman sat with her memories in this room, so alive with the presence of her mother. 'You must miss her.'

'I miss her every day,' Marguerite replied. 'But there is suffering worse that the loss of someone you love ...' A harrowed expression fell upon her face as if a storm cloud had crossed her mind. 'And that is bearing the burden of responsibility for death oneself.'

Megan was taken aback by her words, confused. For a moment she thought her own secret was laid unexpectedly bare. Yet Marguerite was speaking of herself. The truth of her words moved Megan to confess.

'I know it,' she said.

'Do you?' Marguerite was shaken from her own melancholy.

'Yes,' said Megan with shame. 'I do.'

Without another word Marguerite searched for Megan's hand, pulled it into the folds of the primrose silk and clasped her fingers tight.

Marguerite didn't appear downstairs the following day until Megan saw her at dusk, standing by the kitchen door, tense and trembling as if in a trance.

'Is something wrong?' Megan asked.

'They're out there,' hissed Marguerite. 'Watching.'

Megan went to the window but she could see no one in the yard.

'They're fools to think night will hide them from us. We see them, skulking in the shadows.'

Megan could see and hear nothing. She opened the door and slipped outside. Something caught her eye, darting across the gloom of the stable. Warily she tiptoed towards it, determined to look, prepared to run. Maybe someone had come for her after all. But as she reached the door a loud shriek from within sent her fleeing back to the house.

'It's the birds,' she said, catching her breath. 'They're in the stables.'

But Marguerite waved her hand in protest. 'They were there.' she said faintly. 'They whisper curses. I hear them, sons and wives, mothers and daughters … they'll never, ever forget.'

She reached out an arm for Megan who helped her to walk, unsteadily to the staircase. Then, she disappeared once more to her room.

As the days passed, Megan became accustomed to Marguerite's strange obsessions. But the oppressive heat outside and the atmosphere of fearful suspicion in the house made her tense. Although Megan was no longer terrified that the owls would harm her, she was still afraid of the menace in their eyes, their silent intelligence. She felt they wanted something from her. Whenever she left the house, to take a walk or fetch milk from the farm, they followed. Sometimes she saw them, perching on a gate or fencepost nearby, sometimes she just sensed their presence. But whenever they were close she felt the eyes of Marguerite upon her. To her alarm, Marguerite did often seem to know where Megan had been. She knew when Megan had searched along the stream for watercress, when she'd walked in the wood and even once how she'd helped to catch a foal at Tawks Farm.

In the house, Marguerite rang for Megan at any hour of the day or night. Even though she had an acute awareness of what Megan did, she was oddly confused about time and her appetite was as erratic as her sleep. Megan did her best to have food prepared for whenever Marguerite might call and sometimes the blind woman was grateful, but other times she was cold and aloof. What Megan found most disturbing of all was Marguerite's habit of suddenly falling silent and still, almost as if she were in a trance, and staring into the distance. Sometimes this lasted for seconds, sometimes three or four minutes. At first Megan thought she was ill. Then the episode would pass and Marguerite would continue her sentence or her passage through the room as if nothing had happened, as if she had momentarily slipped out of the world to another place and back again, without expecting anyone to notice.

One evening, to Megan's horror, the birds appeared downstairs. Marguerite brought them to the parlour, where they stood on the table with intimidating presence.

'What scraps can you bring them?' Marguerite asked as she stroked the breast of the nearest owl. The bird inclined its head towards her, eyes half-closed. With a scratch of claws the second owl shifted unsteadily on the polished wood.

'What do they eat?' asked Megan.

'Chicken heads, feet and gizzard ...,' said Marguerite softly, dusting the broad wings with the back of her hand. 'Anything that won't go into the pot.'

Megan was repulsed by the sight and smell of the birds, cloistered in that dark, airless room. They stared, unblinking, into her soul. What did they hunt for? Some knowledge, some conspiracy of fate that would give them possession of her ...

'There's nothing left today,' she mumbled, taking a step away. Marguerite fixed Megan with her blank eyes.

'Don't let them see you're afraid,' she said. The bird

beneath her fingers edged closer and began pecking at her collar as if preening its own plumage. Marguerite slowly closed her hand over its head and pushed it away. At once both birds shrieked and flapped in agitation, fluttering awkwardly beyond the candle's pool of light to hide in the dark depths of the room.

Megan hurried out of the parlour but a moment later the owls swooped after her, one by one. Their broad wings filled the kitchen, beating the air in a commotion of white feathers above her head. She screamed and ran into the buttery. As soon as she was gone the birds fell silent. She peered around the doorway. They were perched together between the copper pans on a high shelf – settled, like poachers in a hide, to watch and wait. It was some time before Megan dared to return to the room. When she did, the birds seemed to be asleep. Nervously, Megan cleared the cooking things from the table, trying to avoid turning her back on them, then she climbed up to the loft, pulling an old rug she'd found across the opening after her. There she lay uneasily, listening to the scuffles and scratching from the kitchen below.

From that night the owls extended their territory to hers. In the following days they came and went, like their mistress, unbothered by the hour. Sometimes one would trap Megan in a doorway, challenging her to pass. But she was too afraid to edge around it. Sometimes one would alight on the table, claiming whatever dish or spoon she needed, as if it knew her every thought. They'd be watching when she found feathers and pellets among the kitchen things and once, to her horror, a small, mutilated creature. They were testing her nerve. Drinking her fear with their black eyes.

At night, Jacob soared through her dreams – his frail, white wings never strong enough to fly free, always spinning hopelessly, spiralling down to lie lifeless, like a crumpled fledgling, at her feet.

Megan began to feel suffocated by this strange existence with Marguerite and, although she had been afraid of contact, of questions, she now longed for someone to talk to. Nobody in the village would give her more than a curt 'good day'.

Every few days Jack Sharpe brought a basket of food from Tawks Farm, as his wife had promised. If Megan left a note in the empty crock asking for eggs, or a twist of cinnamon, her request was always answered, but no matter how early she rose she never once caught sight of him. It was only when she went to the farm herself that Megan found any friendship, for the farmer's wife seemed to like her, or feel sorry for her, at least. She would often give Megan something warm from the stove and, once, a dress and a pair of boots left by her daughter who lived far away. But although she seemed to look kindly upon Megan she would not be drawn into much conversation and never any tale regarding Marguerite or the Manor. Always the owls watched over them, perched on the weathervane or the long barn roof. Always the farmer's wife turned her back to them.

'I'm as superstitious as any,' she said. 'Those birds prey on sorrow. They bring no good.'

Day by day Megan felt more curious, more afraid and more alone.

Nine

Tom

The hot weather continued, but summer was dying. Change was in the air.

Megan was sitting at the kitchen table peeling potatoes one morning when a waft of smoke drifted through the open window. She hurried outside to save the washing she'd hung up earlier from the taint of smoke, wondering if someone had lit a bonfire close to the house. But as she reached the back garden she saw a tide of flame advancing across the stubble-field beyond, burning away the barley stalks, leaving the land scorched black. Megan quickly unpegged the damp clothes from the washing line and ran with them back into the house. She left the heap on the table and went out again to watch over the hedge, fascinated by the drama of the fire. The dry stalks crackled as the fire devoured them, spitting out sparks and billowing grey smoke which trailed and twined like tresses of breeze-blown hair. Two farmhands shepherded the flames with their rakes while two more behind them scuffed out the embers as they stamped across the hot earth. The four men didn't seem to be in control of it, she thought, but as if they were the fire's attendants. Megan felt its elemental power. She imagined that ragged ribbon of flame relentlessly circling the world, never extinguished, but rolling on and on, year after year – destroying everything in its path. It was hard to believe green shoots would grow again one day in that burnt place.

Suddenly the smoke caught her throat. She coughed and pulled her apron up to cover her mouth. As she raised her head she noticed a boy standing at the field gate, watching the spectacle. Tall and skinny, still as a statue, he looked older than Megan and seemed transfixed. He held a long stick, spear-like at his side and from his fist hung a dead rabbit. The smoke caught the back of Megan's throat once more and made her choke loudly. The boy turned towards her. Megan rubbed her eyes. When she opened them again he was gone. She looked beyond the gate. It opened onto a lane that ran beside the churchyard, but there was no sign of the boy, either among the yew trees or the tombstones.

Megan wondered about him. He had an air, as if he'd been plucked from some other place, as if he was lost. But then everything in Morne seemed lost.

She turned back to look at the bright tongues of fire feasting on the barley stalks.

A while later, Megan brought the washing back out to finish drying. A grey cat jumped off the stone bench into her path and Megan bent to stroke it. The cat rubbed its thin body against her skirts, weaving back and forth, but as Megan raised her hand to pet it the cat bounded off towards the farmyard. It paused in the archway for a moment and gazed back.

'Come, pusskin,' said Megan softly, but it ran off again. Megan followed it into the yard. And there was the boy, standing in the gateway, still carrying his stick, with the limp rabbit hanging at his side. The cat ran straight to him.

The boy stared at Megan. His eyes were dark as violets, his skin nut-brown and his thick hair long and wild. He wore a sleeveless leather jerkin, many sizes too big for him, over a dirty smock and battered boots laced with twine. Despite his tramp-like appearance he stood with his feet squarely planted in the dry dust and his chin raised as if, for all the world, he was master of the place.

'What do you want?' said Megan.

The boy ignored her question. Without taking his eyes off Megan, he opened his jerkin and thrust the rabbit into a large pocket. The cat wove itself around his legs and purred loudly. Megan met the boy's eyes defiantly.

'What do you want?' she repeated.

The boy crouched down to stroke the cat. 'Do you live here?' he asked.

'Yes.'

He ran his hand along the cat's back and up its stiff, raised tail. For a moment he said nothing but seemed to consider them both. Then he smiled at Megan.

'Come on, stroke it,' he said. 'You want to, don't you? Come on, then it'll know you when I'm gone.'

Megan felt the pull of companionship from the cat and the boy. Shyly she crossed the yard, knelt beside them and rubbed the cat between its ears. It trembled with hunger, tormented by the smell of the rabbit.

'What's your name?' asked Megan, noticing his calloused hands and bitten nails.

'Tom. What's yours, then?'

'Megan.'

Tom gently lifted the cat onto his knees. At once it tried to burrow into his jacket. Megan had to shuffle a little closer to reach it. She smelt the smoke on the boy.

'Fetch it some milk, Megan,' said Tom. 'You've got milk?'

'No one feeds a wild cat,' said Megan. 'It'll never hunt for itself.'

'Go on, give it a dish of milk,' said Tom. 'It's only young. It's a loner, look. A poor orphan.'

Megan noticed a teasing glint in Tom's eye. 'You don't know that,' she said. 'It just wants your rabbit.'

'That's my supper,' said Tom. He patted the bulky shape in his pocket. 'Come and cook it for me.'

Megan felt her cheeks flame at his suggestion. But she liked him for wanting to be friends. 'Where's your home?'

'I don't have one. I'm just passing through. On my own,

like the cat,' he said. 'I've pitched up in an empty house down at the west end of the village. Look ...' He pulled a handful of fat carrots out of his pocket. 'I'll cook him up with these.' Megan picked out a carrot that had split, half way down, into two roots like a pair of legs.

'That's a rider,' said Tom. One leg was bent as if it was about to leap up. Tom made it dance on Megan's hand.

'Why do you call it that?' she asked.

'Because it's been riding a flint, see,' said Tom. 'Straddling it like a farm boy on a cart horse.'

Megan smiled shyly.

Tom stood up and let the cat slip from his arms. 'Go find yourself a mouse,' he said. 'I'm hungry too.' He picked up his stick. 'Come on, then, Meggie. Just for a while. And I'll show you something ...'

Megan's heart skipped a beat. Only Jacob ever called her Meggie. From across the yard she heard the sound of a latch being lifted at the garret window. She ground her fingers into her palms, tempted to go with him, yet afraid of what might happen. 'No, no ... I can't,' she stuttered. 'I'm sorry ... I can't come away!' Grabbing her skirts she ran back to the house.

Ten

Camp

Megan couldn't get Tom out of her head. She sat in the shade of the cowshed next morning rolling an ear of wheat between her hands, wishing she'd been bold enough to go with him. Her palms prickled from the hard, dry grains. As she blew away the chaff, the little grey cat appeared from nowhere. It slipped under the gate, yawned and stretched in the sun, then strolled over to her.

'Where's the rabbit boy?' Megan said quietly. 'You know, don't you?' She reached out to stroke it, as Tom had done, but the fickle cat took a step away, paused to brush its ears and walked off.

Megan stood up and shook the dust from her skirt. The owls, preening themselves on a cartwheel nearby, stopped burrowing into their feathers to watch her. They knew. They knew who she was thinking about. And they knew how she hated them.

Suddenly the birds heard something and flew off. A few minutes later a horse and cart rumbled past the yard gate. Megan recognised it at once from Tawks Farm. The man at the reins, dressed in his Sunday suit, must be Jack Sharpe, she guessed. In the back of the cart was a coffin with an empty canary cage sitting on top. Megan remembered the disgruntled old man who had quizzed her. There would be no more smoke rings in East End, she thought sadly.

Later that evening, when Megan was in the kitchen, she saw the lean, stark silhouette of the boy in the field behind the house. At once she blew out her rush light. But when she looked again he was gone.

Megan sensed it was best to say nothing about Tom to Marguerite and so she kept their meeting to herself.

67

However, as she laid cutlery on the table the following day, Marguerite grabbed her by the wrist.

'Who is the boy who watches the house?'

Megan tried to wrench her hand free but Marguerite snatched the other one.

'I don't know!' She struggled but Marguerite's grip was strong. 'I don't know about a boy.'

Marguerite squeezed tighter and pulled her close. 'We don't need anyone here, you and I. We don't want questions.' Megan felt panic rise in her throat. She tried to evade the stare of Marguerite's wild, blank eyes.

'We've seen him – at the gate, in the yard. Watching,' she hissed. 'He has come to make trouble. You must send him away!' She released Megan's hands and sank back in her chair.

Megan rubbed her wrists and stared at Marguerite. She must have heard Tom's voice in the yard the day before, but she couldn't have seen anyone watching the house. It must be her imagination. And yet Megan had felt herself watched, she'd seen his figure in the dark . . .

'Why should anyone make trouble here?' she said.

'Trouble was made in this place years ago.' Marguerite sighed deeply. 'It still bides here, brooding in the minds of those that never forget.'

Megan was angry that she'd been hurt. Why was Marguerite so afraid? She had no reason to fear Tom – he wasn't from the village, he was just passing through. Maybe while he was here he might even help at the house. He could chop firewood and fix things up a little. If only Marguerite wasn't so suspicious. She looked at the blind woman, locked away once more in her private world. The following day Megan decided to find Tom.

She didn't need to look hard. Megan was winding up the bucket at the well when she heard a scraping sound in the lane. She set the full bucket on the ground and walked quietly through the yard. One of the owls was perched on the gate, toying with a limp mouse between its claws. As Megan reached the lane, the other bird landed beside it and tried to snatch the mouse away. She looked up and down the road. There was no one to be seen except an old dame scolding a scrawny dog as she hobbled up her garden path, but Megan noticed someone had opened the door to the smithy. She crossed the lane and peered in at the door.

Tom stood by the anvil, weighing a long iron in his hand, his pockets bulging with nails.

'The girl who ran away!' he said, looking up. Megan could hardly see Tom's face in the darkness but she could hear his smirk.

'I didn't run away. I had things to do.'

Tom shrugged and turned his attention to the blacksmith's tools. He spotted a hammer, which he slid into the pocket inside his jerkin, then helped himself to some thatching pins. 'What's up?' he said when he caught Megan watching. 'They're here for the taking, aren't they?'

'I suppose so,' she said. 'It's a strange, broken down place, this village.' Tom huffed as if it was of no interest to him. He took a step towards her, slipping half his body into the curtain of light from the door.

'Do you like ferrets?' he said.

'Yes,' she answered, although she'd never seen one.

'Come on then,' he said. 'You'll come this time, won't you?' Megan had never met anyone so direct, so sure of himself before.

She looked over his shoulder at the birds outside, watching her from the yard. 'Yes,' she said. 'I'll come.'

Tom was pleased. 'You'll see, I'll show you something amazing!'

Megan followed Tom through the village, his jerkin full of ironware rattling like a tinker's bag. They took a path that led up to the church. Megan thought he moved like a fox, tramping, head crouched into his shoulders, eyes darting left and right, constantly scanning – for what she could not guess. Two ancient yew trees flanked the graveyard, which was untended and overgrown. Tom hurried silently through the long grass, past a patch of bare ground, which was the only evidence of the burial the day before. At the sight of the freshly dug grave Megan stopped. She stared at the footprints around it and her own bare feet beside. All at once she was standing at Jacob's grave again, in the grey rain. A huddle of mourners was gathered, but no one offered her a word or gesture of comfort. Cruellest of all was her parents' silence. They stood apart, without a word of acknowledgment, leaving Megan to bear her grief alone. Unable to lift her eyes from the ground, she watched her tears mingle with the rain, turning the trampled earth to mud.

Now, once more, Megan felt the weight of that grief, the guilt-stone so heavy in her heart. She wished she could sink into the mud and be swallowed into the grave herself ...

She was struck by something that had never occurred to her before, something missing – there had been no bird. Birds had come for the other babies when they died, but for Jacob there had been no bird. Why, she wondered?

'Come on, Meggie. Are you following?' Tom sat on a stile cut in the far wall of the graveyard, swinging his legs.

Megan turned to him. 'Don't call me that!' she cried sharply. 'Don't ever call me that!'

Tom was startled. He frowned and muttered something. Then he dropped over the stile and disappeared. Megan stared after him. Why had she said that? Why give herself away? She hurried after him.

When Megan caught up with Tom he was snapping a long stem of dry grass in his fingers. He handed her one the same. For a while they walked along in silence. Then Tom spotted a robin's pincushion on a bush.

'So, who calls you Meggie?' he asked, as he poked at it with his stick.

'My brother did,' mumbled Megan.

'Did?' Tom caught the mossy scarlet bundle in his hand.

'He died,' said Megan. 'Not so long ago. That's why I stopped at that grave. It just reminded me, that's all.' Her voice faltered.

'How did it happen?'

She couldn't answer. She wasn't ready. But Tom persisted with his questions. 'Did he get sick?'

Megan nodded, hoping he would ask no more.

Tom rolled the pincushion in his hand as if turning a thought in his mind, then dropped it onto the toe of his boot and kicked it high over the hedge. 'Well, if we're going to be friends I'll call you Meg.'

Megan had the uncomfortable feeling that Tom was claiming her in some way with the name. Yet it felt good to walk with him. She had come so far alone. From the bank of a brook nearby a heron took flight, rising strong, slow and sure.

'I don't mind,' she said, watching the bird fly off over the water meadow, over the treetops and out of sight. 'Meg is fine, if you like.'

They walked beside a long hedge, through a scrubby field of thistle and gorse. Megan followed Tom, breathing in the scent of coconut that the warm sun drew from the gorse flowers.

'Why have you come here?' she asked.

Tom paused to pick a handful of blackberries. He

brushed away a spider and handed her the plumpest. 'I'm just passing through.'

'So am I,' said Megan. 'I'm only staying a while. But where are you going?'

'Don't know yet,' he replied. 'I've something to do first.' He stuffed the rest of the berries into his mouth and, reaching for a familiar foothold in the wall, climbed over. 'Tell me about that house, the Manor. Who lives there?'

'Just one woman, all on her own. Marguerite, she's called.' Megan heaved herself over the wall after him. 'She's blind.'

Tom stopped abruptly and turned about. 'Why?' he snapped.

Megan thought this was an odd question. 'I don't know,' she said. 'I haven't asked her.'

'You must,' he said. 'Don't you want to know?'

Megan glanced about her. The owls were nowhere in sight, yet she knew they were not far away, watching, listening. 'Well, yes, I suppose I do,' she said quietly, 'but I couldn't ask her. She's quite ... well, there's something strange about her – the way she moves and speaks.' Megan heard a rustle in the tree above. 'It must be awful, living on your own like that.'

'I'd ask her,' said Tom.

'I couldn't. Anyway, I don't see much of her, she only comes downstairs for meals.'

Now Tom was walking close beside Megan, stabbing the ground with his stick as he listened. 'There's no farm or land, then?'

'No. She said she gave it away, the best of it.'

Tom nudged her and pointed to a hole in the hedge nearby. 'Come on, here it is.' Megan followed him through the gap into an overgrown orchard.

Beyond the orchard was a derelict cottage whose roof had fallen in on one side and half the walls collapsed underneath. Tom climbed through an empty window into the only room that remained intact and helped Megan in after him. 'Home sweet home!' he said with a bow. Megan looked around at his few belongings. Against one wall was a bed of dry straw and sacking, beside it a bundle of kindling. A few stubby candle ends were set into the ground.

'Very grand,' she said with a curtsey, and he looked pleased.

Tom gathered an armful of sticks and Megan followed him outside again. He threw them down and set about emptying his pockets. From one came the blacksmith's hammer and nails, from another a rabbit and some vegetables, finally a tinderbox, which he used to make a fire. Megan remembered with embarrassment how long she'd taken to light a fire at the Manor. She watched Tom skin the rabbit and fix up a spit so he could roast it with a couple of potatoes and an apple. He worked purposefully and fast, as if he'd been living that way for some time. He was sure of himself. Older than his years, she felt. Although he'd looked scrawny beneath his oversized jerkin she saw now that he was wiry and strong. If I was a boy I could survive alone like this, she thought, jealously. But then if she were a boy she wouldn't have had to run away ...

Tom slapped the handle of his knife into her hand and tossed a bunch of carrots into her lap. 'You trim them. I'll fill the pot,' and he picked up a jug and disappeared off.

When he returned with the jug full of water Tom also carried a cage under his arm.

'Here he is. Hungry too, eh!' He lifted the door and a brown ferret ran straight up his arm and nuzzled excitedly around his collar. Megan stretched out her hand to stroke it.

'Mind yourself,' warned Tom. 'He's a nasty nip.'

'What's his name?'

'He doesn't need one,' Tom laughed. The ferret tumbled down Tom's other arm and scampered over to sniff Megan's hand. 'Just let him come to you, but keep him away from your face.'

Megan kept quite still. And to her delight, while Tom fetched some food, the ferret leapt and somersaulted in the folds of her skirt.

Tom produced a dead mouse and some fruit, which the ferret ate hungrily. Then he lifted it back into its cage,

where it curled up to lick its face and paws and, after a
while, fell asleep.

Tom settled himself by the fire beside Megan and found a
stick to poke at the ash as they watched the meat darken
and crisp.

She remembered Tom's promise. 'You were going to
show me something amazing.'

Tom smiled. 'Yes, you'll like it!' He stabbed the end of
his stick into the fire and scrambled back into the cottage,
emerging a moment later with a calico bag from which he
pulled a tuft of soft, wispy stuff.

'What's that?' asked Megan.

'Old man's beard. Watch . . .' Tom laid it out on the palm
of his hand and tugged the stick from the fire. As he touched
the silky threads with the glowing end of the stick they
prickled with sparks, floating up into the air like dancing
fireflies, and then disappeared.

Megan was entranced. She begged him to do it again.

Daylight was fading and the flying sparks lit their faces
with a thousand tiny living lights. Tom's eyes blazed. For a
moment Megan felt her heart stir.

A flutter of wings startled her. Two hunched shapes
settled side by side on the branch of a dead tree nearby.
She scrambled to her feet nervously. They'd come for
her. Marguerite would know and she wouldn't like
it.

'I have to go,' she said. 'I have to go back now. It'll soon be dark and I don't have a lantern.'

'But there'll be food enough for two,' protested Tom. Then he saw the owls, bronzed by the firelight like two ancient statues. At once he bounded over to the sleeping ferret and shut its cage door. 'Do you see them?' he whispered, pointing at the birds. 'I've watched them, by your house. It's not natural the way they come and go.' Megan wanted to tell Tom about the owls but she saw he was afraid for his ferret. If he knew they followed her he might not let her return.

'I must go back to Marguerite,' she said. 'She'll be needing me.'

Tom reached out and grabbed Megan by the wrist, just as Marguerite had done. 'Don't tell her I'm here, Meg. Don't tell her about me.'

Megan pulled away from him. 'No, I won't if you don't want me to.'

She went back through the orchard and searched for the place they'd climbed through the hedge. Tom was quickly at her side.

'Here ...' He showed her the way.

Without a word Megan ducked through the gap and turned towards the church.

As Tom watched Megan leave, the owls swooped low over his head and followed her home.

That night, Tom lay propped on his elbow by the dying embers of his fire, teasing the ferret with a piece of straw poked through the wire mesh of its cage.

'That girl, Meg, she likes you and me,' he said, as the ferret batted the straw with its paws. 'We'll keep friendly with her, eh? She could be useful when the time comes. Maybe she's just what we need.'

Eleven

Eyes

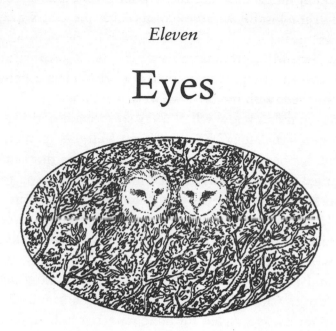

When Megan returned to the Manor the bell rang almost immediately. She lit a candle and went to the parlour but Marguerite wasn't sitting in her usual place at the table. A chair moved in the darkness at the far end of the room and Marguerite spoke.

'Come here, to me.' Her voice was taut. Megan approached, shaking so much that she made the candlelight shudder across the walls. Marguerite sat, white fists clenched in her lap. She stared blindly at Megan, across the flame.

'We've been waiting. We know where you have been.'

All the way home Megan had dreaded this but she hadn't forgotten her promise to Tom. 'I went for a walk,' she said, 'and I got lost. But there's yesterday's pie. I'll warm it straightaway.'

'So, you will lie to me.'

Her words stung. Megan could not help feeling ashamed.

'You went with the boy. We were watching.'

Megan didn't know what to say so she said nothing.

'You left me alone.' For a moment Marguerite made no sound, her head swayed curiously back and forth, then she breathed deeply. 'My friends tell me he tempted you to sit at his fireside, to share his food? And he had a creature ... you held it. What did the boy ask you? What did you say?'

Marguerite's words frightened Megan. How could she know? How could Marguerite know about Tom and the fire and the food? How could she possibly know about the ferret? Close by, the hunched birds murmured like conspirators. Megan felt the blind woman's hold upon her; knowledge and will binding her close.

'I didn't mean to be so long ...'

'I told you we see everything, Megan,' said Marguerite softly. 'We don't like strangers, do we? Don't speak to him again.'

'But ...'

'We are sufficient for each other, you and I.' Marguerite rubbed her temples wearily. 'Bring me supper now. I am weak from distress.'

When Megan went up to bed in the apple loft later that evening she found that her mattress had been ripped in several places, the straw pulled out and scattered across the floor. Choked with indignation, she gathered the straw, stuffed it back inside and turned the meagre mattress over. But it served as little comfort.

All that night she tossed and turned restlessly. Jacob ran through the moonlit garden, weeping, thrusting his arms to the sky. Above, circled a commotion of blind owls and among them loomed Marguerite, staring with the all-seeing, unblinking gaze of the birds. How could these creatures be her eyes? It couldn't be true. And yet Marguerite knew things, things that were surely impossible for her to know.

Twelve

Ghosts

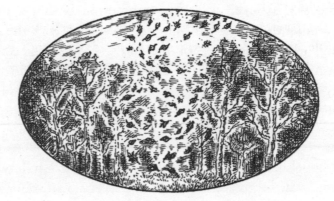

Next morning, Megan was still upset and angry that Marguerite had forbidden her to talk to Tom. I have to see him again, she thought. In the few hours they'd spent together she had felt something unfamiliar about herself, brighter and unafraid. He knows nothing about me; he doesn't need to know. She could be whoever she wanted to be in his company.

She didn't want to upset Marguerite. After all, Tom was only staying awhile and he might be gone tomorrow. If she displeased Marguerite she might lose the strange security she had found at the Manor. Although it had been hard at first doing the job of maid and cook, work she'd not been born to, she'd grown accustomed to Marguerite's needs and her unpredictable moods. I have food and lodgings here, I can even put up with the birds, Megan thought. If she turned me out I would have nothing. I can't let Tom spoil things.

Megan found a needle and cotton and stitched up her mattress as best she could. With every stitch she mulled over what to do.

The strong, coarse fabric was difficult to sew without a thimble, and the apple loft was stuffy and hot in the middle of the day. When she'd finished Megan went out into the garden for some air.

As she walked in the shade of the house Megan ran her hand through the spires of a rosemary bush. At once the scent reminded her of home – of Cook's herbal rinses and how she would sometimes wash Megan's hair with rosemary water to cheer her up. 'We'll have you shiny as a chestnut,' Cook would say.

Megan decided to make some rosemary water for herself. She picked a handful of leaves and carried them inside. As the herbs steeped in a pan of boiled water their pungent smell pervaded the house and drew Marguerite to the kitchen. To Megan's relief Marguerite's outburst of the previous day seemed forgotten and Megan explained what she planned to do with the herbs.

Apart from talking to strangers, Marguerite did not seemed bothered by what Megan did when she wasn't attending to her duties. She rubbed a rosemary stem between her fingers and held it to her nose. 'We always used camomile,' she said wistfully.

Megan looked at her white hair, pinned in elaborate, untidy curls, several of which had fallen from their pins and tumbled about her neck. 'Would you like me to wash your hair?' she asked nervously. At once Marguerite smiled. The smile lifted her face and for a brief moment care slipped away. For the first time Megan realised that she was not an old woman at all.

Later that day, Megan heated water in the kitchen and washed Marguerite's hair, using some tallow soap she'd got from Jack Sharpe. Marguerite sat, eyes shut, with her head rested back over the basin. As Megan gently massaged the soapy lather into her damp curls she felt the blind woman's trust in her – just as Jacob had trusted her to catch him or nurse him without a care. There was something childlike about Marguerite too, Megan thought. Her simple needs, her dependence. The way her moods changed. She seemed most alive in her memories of childhood.

'Do you have any family?' Megan asked, rinsing the soap away.

'Brothers or sisters? No. Not even cousins.' Marguerite shifted uneasily in her chair. 'Maybe if I had I wouldn't have been so doted on. It makes one vain and selfish. And if I hadn't been so selfish all would be different. My father would still be here, mother would be alive and I would have eyes to see them.'

Megan didn't know what to say. She reached for the jug of rosemary water. 'Was your mother ... did she ... ?'

'She died of a broken heart.' Marguerite pulled a handkerchief from her sleeve to mop her wet brow.

'I didn't know people really could die that way.' Megan thought of her grief-stricken parents, who'd hardly stirred from their separate rooms since Jacob died.

'It's true. Without my father she lost any reason to live.'

'But you were still there,' blurted Megan.

'Yes,' said Marguerite. 'I was there, but I was not enough.'

Not enough. Megan had felt the same. She gently squeezed the water from Marguerite's hair and wrapped a towel around it. Not enough to live for, just like me. She dug her nails hard into her palms.

Marguerite clutched the towel, rising unsteadily from her awkward position and Megan helped her to a chair at the hearth.

How can you believe in yourself when you're not enough to live for?

A few days later, when Megan went to fetch wood from the shed, she was surprised to see Tom at the yard gate, frowning. He seemed to be studying something she couldn't see. Megan watched how still and alert he stood, like a cat about to pounce. She admired him for being his own master, answering to no one, belonging to no one. Unafraid and independent, he was so different to anyone she had ever met. What strange company, she thought – this boy, alive as a wild thing and Marguerite, fading alone in the dark.

Megan stepped through the archway into the yard but Tom still didn't notice her. He was mesmerised by the owls, perched like sentinels on the wall. The birds and the boy stared at each other so intently it seemed to Megan as if some unuttered exchange was passing between them. For a moment Megan was afraid to disturb him. Then she shifted her foot and kicked a stone across the grass. At once the birds took flight. Tom turned on his heel. The scowl on his face fell away when he saw her.

'I was coming for you, Meg!' he said with a smile. 'Walk with me up to the woods.'

Now Megan felt the scrutiny of his eyes upon her. She smiled at his directness, not asking but commanding. So sure of himself.

One of the owls took off from the wall and flew to the ledge of the open attic window, where it ducked its head and slipped into the dark room. The second bird followed, but it paused on the threshold, flexing its wings. Slowly it twisted its head towards Megan in the yard below. It locked its steady gaze upon her for a long moment, then turned dismissively and hopped inside. Tom watched in astonishment.

Megan walked over to him without looking back. 'She knows about you,' Megan said. 'I didn't tell. She must have heard us with the cat the other day.'

'She doesn't know anything about me!' Tom retorted. A twitch of the scowl creased his face briefly, then the smile returned. 'Are you coming?'

Megan stepped closer, tense and unsure. 'She told me I wasn't to see you again.'

'So?' Tom shrugged. 'You said she needs you. She isn't going to turn you out, is she?'

'I've got nowhere else to go. I don't want to cross her.'

'Come on,' Tom scuffed the dirt impatiently. 'Didn't you say she sleeps in the day?'

'There's no pattern to it,' said Megan. 'She calls me at any hour. I think she hardly sleeps at all.'

'Is she mad?'

'No, don't say that. She knows what's happening. She knew about you and the fire and cooking the rabbit. She even knows about the ferret.'

'How could she?'

Megan nodded towards the attic window. 'The birds ... she says they're her eyes.'

Tom grinned uneasily. 'Crazy witch!' he cried loudly and grabbed Megan's hand. Megan winced and jerked her hand away. At once Tom saw her palm criss-crossed with fresh white wheals.

'How did you do that?' He took both hands and turned them over.

'It's nothing.' Megan snatched them away again. She felt ashamed. Sometimes she didn't even realise what she had done. 'Just some stingers. It doesn't hurt.'

Tom knew very well that it did. 'Rub dock on them,' he said. 'There must be some growing here ...' He searched the weeds around them.

'Look, I don't care!' Megan snapped. 'I hate my hands!' She glanced back at the house defiantly. 'Come on, show me the woods.' Before he could ask any more questions she dashed out of the yard ahead of him.

Megan and Tom ran and didn't stop until they reached the drove path Megan had taken the night she came over the Downs. Tom slumped against a tree to catch his breath. Megan, a few steps behind dropped onto her knees beside him.

'Do you think Marguerite heard what you called her?' Megan panted.

'Who cares?' jeered Tom.

'But what will I say when I go back?'

'You'll think of something. Or does she know your thoughts as well?'

Now it was Megan's turn to scowl. 'You're teasing me,' she said.

'No. I'm interested.' Tom paused a moment as if to emphasise this point then he scrambled to his feet. 'Tell me about her. Tell me everything.' He started up the track. Megan followed him.

As they walked on up the path Tom asked endless questions about Marguerite, about her habits and the Manor House itself. Most of all he asked about the owls. 'I don't like birds,' he said. 'My brother was a scarer. All day rattlin' and hollerin' from field to field. He knew how to deal with them, a mob of gulls or murder of crows. And he'd never eat a feathered thing, not even a squab in a pie.

Birds like those owls could scratch your eyes out.'

'Don't!' said Megan in horror. 'They follow me everywhere.'

'Maybe they took out her eyes?'

'No,' said Megan. 'She has eyes, all white and milky. She stares as if she's looking inside you, or as if a ghost is looking out of her.'

'That'd be right,' said Tom gruffly.

'What do you mean?'

'Ghosts. I bet she's haunted by them.' Tom swiped at a low-slung branch with his stick.

'Do you believe in them?' asked Megan, falling in step behind him as the track narrowed.

'Course I do. They're dead people that get trapped in between here and there,' said Tom. 'They can't rest until things are settled. You have to help them pass on. You have to make some reck'ning to square things.'

'I don't understand,' said Megan. But Tom just swiped his stick at the long grass and remained silent. I wish my mind was as sure and strong as his, she thought. She clenched her throbbing fists.

'I'm haunted by a ghost.' The words escaped her mouth strangled and strange. 'I'm haunted by my brother.'

Tom walked on as if he hadn't heard her.

'He comes into my dreams.' Megan struggled to control her voice. 'And he's always crying. He won't let me go.'

Tom slowed down as the track began to rise steeply and turned to her with a grim face. Megan stopped. He looked down at her but Megan had the oddest feeling that he wasn't seeing her at all. 'It's not the dead ones that won't let go,' he said. 'They can't have a hold on you. It's the other way, see? That's how it is.'

Megan didn't understand Tom's words but she recognised the hardness in his voice. A hardness that protected him from feeling. She wondered if he, too, had a stone in his heart ...

Tom reached out and took her by the arm, to help her up the rise. They spoke no more of ghosts.

A short distance further the ground fell sharply away on one side of the path, into a deep chalk pit. Tom turned away from it and skirted around the top edge of the wood. As they rose out of the hollow into sunlight his mood lifted. 'Ever caught a squirrel, Meg?' he asked.

'No, I can't climb a tree,' said Megan. Tom laughed loudly. But his laugh was not unkind. It melted the awkwardness between them.

'Anyone can climb a tree,' he said. 'You could if you wanted to. But you don't catch a squirrel like that. Look.' He pulled a stone with a hole through it out of his pocket. 'You use a stone stick, see.' He stopped and searched around under the trees for a stick and pushed the stone on the end of it. 'Now, we mustn't make a sound, understand? And watch your feet. Follow me ...'

Megan marvelled at how silent Tom could be in his big boots. He led her through the undergrowth, stopping suddenly now and then, to watch and listen. They found a clearing and he gestured to her to crouch down at the edge of it. They watched a long while, still and close, until Megan's legs began to ache. At last something rustled above their heads. She saw a hunched red back and a feathery tail dart along a branch. Tom waited until the squirrel stopped to examine the nut in its paws. Then, with a whip of his arm the stone shot silently through the air and the squirrel dropped onto the leaves below.

Tom leapt out of the undergrowth and found the squirrel at once. He weighed the little body in his hand for meat and stowed it in his pocket.

'Didn't your brother teach you stuff?' Tom asked as they sat in the branches of an oak tree a while later. He had found an easy foothold for Megan, who'd heaved herself onto a low, broad branch. Now she leaned against the trunk, swinging her feet, exhilarated by the leafy world that surrounded her.

'He was younger than me. Only six,' she said.

'No sisters?' asked Tom.

'No. No one else.' Megan didn't want to talk about herself any more. She slipped off the branch awkwardly and kicked up a drift of rusty leaves below.

'Don't you have family? Who taught you to catch a squirrel?'

'I've brothers, all right. Four. All gone for soldiers,' said Tom. 'They're gonna send old Boney packing when the invasion comes.' He slashed the branches with an imaginary sword, sending a shower of golden leaves fluttering down around her. Megan swung her arms in the leaf storm.

'Don't you have a mother and father?' she said.

'Don't *you*?' came the quick reply. The leaves settled and the air was still once more.

Megan understood. No more questions. It suited her too. But as they walked to the summit of the down and circled back to the west end of the village, Tom quizzed her again about Marguerite and the Manor, especially about Marguerite's relationship with the birds. It seemed to Megan that this interested him more than anything else they had talked about.

Tom was the first to smell a trace of smoke drifting on the air. 'Let's find it.' He quickened his step.

'Why? It's only a bonfire,' said Megan. But she remembered how Tom had been mesmerised by the stubble burning and the flying sparks of the old man's beard. He was drawn to fire, like a moth. They came to a tiny yellow cottage, built end-on to the lane and found an old man stoking a bonfire in his back garden. Tom stood up close to the fence to watch. The man was lifting a heap of clothes from the grass with a pitchfork and heaving them onto the flames. He eyed Tom and Megan as he paused to wipe the sweat from his face, but didn't acknowledge them. Tom remained unabashed, staring as a shoe, then a bonnet, was flung in after the clothes. Megan was embarrassed. She sensed some private business was taking place. 'Tom,' she hissed under her breath. 'Tom, come away ...'

Suddenly the old man raised the pitchfork towards them and shouted angrily. 'Yaargh! Get outta here! Go to the Devil, or I'll send you meself!' He stamped his boot and waved his fist in the air. Tom remained rooted to the spot, but as Megan turned to run she saw at once that the old man hadn't been shouting at them but at the owls, which had arrived silently and perched on a rowan tree behind her. They flapped their wings in agitation at the old man's fury and swooped away.

'Evil creatures,' the old man muttered to Tom. 'Stay away from them.'

'Why?' said Tom.

'They're bad omens,' said the old man, pulling a neckerchief out of his pocket to wipe his red face. 'Everyone round here knows that. If they come for you there's always disaster'll follow. They came for my May and she fell sick all-a-sudden with fever. That was two weeks past and now I'm burning her things.' He rubbed his eyes with the back of his hand and shook his head.

'Now they come back to gloat over their wicked work.'

Suddenly the heat of the fire and his fury and grief seemed to overcome him. He stumbled and collapsed onto the garden bench. Megan darted towards the gate but he waved her back. 'Pass on, pass on. Let me be.'

Without a word Tom stooped down and picked up a stone. He flung it after the birds but they had long gone. He and Megan walked back to the Manor in silence.

'What'll I say when Marguerite asks me about you?' said Megan as they reached the house.

'Don't say anything,' Tom replied. 'Tell me everything she says. Everything she does, do you hear? Mind those birds, but don't be afraid of her.' He stopped outside the garden door and turned to Megan. 'Don't be afraid, Meg,' he said. 'Remember, you have me now.'

Despite Tom's words, when Marguerite called for her supper that evening Megan was afraid. To her relief, Marguerite asked nothing about where she'd been.

But later that evening when Megan tipped the water pitcher over the kitchen bowl to wash the dishes something wet and dark slid out of its belly. She screamed and almost dropped the jug. Floating on the water was a bedraggled squirrel's tail.

Thirteen

Purse

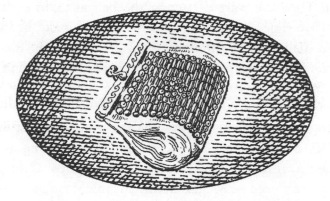

The hot weather continued. Although Megan had the cool refuge of the Manor she had begun to find both the heat outside, and the dark inside, oppressive. She watched out for Tom in the yard. Several times she caught Marguerite standing at a window or door, listening.

'The boy's outside . . .' Marguerite whispered. 'He's there. Watching us. Waiting. Send him away!'

But Megan couldn't send him away. She didn't want to. She arranged a signal with Tom that could be seen from the kitchen window. If the well bucket was turned upside down, he was waiting at the smithy. How he crept through the yard without disturbing the birds she never knew, but she guessed he must watch and wait for them to hunt. When she returned from their walks she always took care to bring in an armful of wood from the shed in case Marguerite was in the kitchen. It was an uncomfortable deception and, day by day, Megan's loyalties grew strained.

Marguerite continued to imagine someone was watching the house, hearing voices and questioning where she had been. Then she started ringing the bell at night – three, four, five times. Each time Megan had to make her way down the ladder in the dark, light a candle from the fire and find Marguerite. At night Marguerite was often in the upstairs drawing room, without fire or candle. Sometimes Megan found her moving chess pieces around a board; other times stitching crazy, chaotic embroideries, with needles she instructed Megan to thread, muttering as she paused to read the stitches with her fingertips. Often she had no real need of Megan at all. She might simply want a question answered or a fallen shawl picked up from the floor. Megan started keeping a lantern alight as best she could, to save herself stumbling down the ladder in the dark. After several nights she was exhausted. Her broken sleep was disturbed by restless dreams of Jacob, flying in dizzy circles about her head, or tugging at her skirts, weeping, always weeping.

Megan began to wake later and later in the morning and fall asleep in the cook's chair in the afternoon. I must stay awake or I shall miss Tom if he comes, she told herself. But each day her exhaustion deepened and she slept a little more. Then, one night a dreadful thought occurred to her. Could Marguerite be trying to keep her away from Tom by forcing Megan into her own weird, nocturnal existence? The more tired and disorientated Megan became, the more convinced she was that it was true. But why did Marguerite want to keep them apart? Was she worried Megan might leave her? Megan remembered Tom's words. 'Don't be afraid, Meg. You have me now.' Yet he seemed to come less often and she wondered how many times she'd missed him. I must see him, she thought desperately. I must find him myself.

As it was, Tom found her, coming boldly into the yard, right up to the kitchen door.

'I've something for you, Meg.' He wouldn't say where he'd been, or what he'd been doing, but he gave Megan a small purse embroidered with blue beads. She opened its tiny gold clasp. Inside, the crimson lining had a faint scent of lavender.

'You do like it, don't you?' he asked earnestly.

'It's so pretty,' said Megan. 'Is it really for me?'

Tom looked pleased. 'It belonged to my mam,' he said. 'You can keep it.' He shifted awkwardly from one foot to the other, still wearing his oversized boots. Megan didn't know what to say. She gave a little curtsey, which made him smile.

Tom stared over her shoulder at the shuttered house. 'Don't she ever go out?' he asked.

'No,' answered Megan, unable to stifle a yawn. 'And

she's got me up in the night so much I'm falling asleep in the day. I think it's her way of stopping me from seeing you.'

'Well, she won't do that, hear me?' said Tom. 'Anyway, it's those birds should be sleeping in the day.' He nodded towards the owls on the ridge of the roof. 'It's not right, the hours they keep.'

Megan turned her back on the birds. 'They're not natural creatures,' she whispered. 'They're like witches' cats, doing her bidding ...'

'Well I hope they fall into her cauldron!' said Tom with a grin. 'Come see me tomorrow. Come and tell me everything then.'

Megan clutched the purse. 'Where are you going now?' She didn't want him to leave so soon.

'I've got something to do, I told you that, didn't I? Don't ask. You'll find out soon enough.'

Fourteen

Help

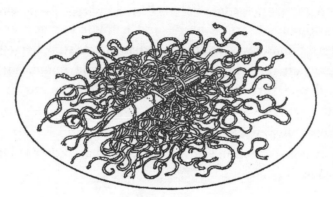

That night Marguerite rang her bell four times. Once so Megan could find a thimble that had dropped under her chair, twice to tell her there was whispering in the yard and the fourth time simply to ask if Mistress Sharpe had made her autumn preserves. As Megan climbed up the loft ladder for the last time she heard a cock crow. Could it really be dawn? She blew out her candle and collapsed onto the bed. Her bones ached and her head swam. I can't do this any more, she thought. Soon I'll live in darkness like Marguerite. My mind is so frayed I'll be mad myself. I have to get away.

Megan thought of Tom. She fumbled for the purse, which she'd hidden beneath the mattress. He had promised to come for her. Maybe he would take her with him when he moved on. She wouldn't care where. He could teach her to get by, how to take care of herself. She'd be safe with him. How she longed to feel truly safe. To sleep without torment. To sleep forever ...

But Megan's mind could not rest. Now she saw a vision of Marguerite, dishevelled, holding out a needle to be threaded. To be alone and helpless – that was the realm of madness. That was what she feared herself. If Megan left the Manor no one else would come. Megan tossed and turned wretchedly. Voices clamoured in her head.

'Step out of the shadow, child. Step out of the dark.'

In the morning Megan sat on the bench outside the kitchen door trying to mend one of Marguerite's skirts. She was so tired that she struggled to keep her eyes open and the work kept falling from her hands. Weak with exhaustion, she began to cry. The cat, which had been washing itself at her feet, pricked up its ears and trotted swiftly towards the farmyard. Megan knew at once Tom was there. Sure enough he leaned against the gatepost, rakishly smoking a chipped clay pipe. Megan laid down her stitching, rubbed her eyes and went to him.

'Did you get your business done?' she asked, feeling the

purse in her pocket. As before, Tom would offer no explanation of where he'd been or what he'd been doing.

'I'm here now, aren't I?' he said. 'Come and help me with something.'

Megan stood in the huge shadow of the house; two familiar but distorted shapes perched on its dark roof. She stepped out of the shadow and was beside him.

Tom grinned and started for the gate.

This is your chance, she told herself silently. Start walking. Save yourself. Don't look back. She began to follow Tom. You just have to go. Don't tell her or she'll persuade you to stay.

It was the only way – just as she'd left home, a lifetime ago. Jack Sharpe would look after Marguerite, as he'd always done. Maybe his wife would take pity and find some other help for her. But Megan's uneasy conscience chanted at every step. No one will come. You know no one will come. What will happen to her?

Megan knew she was needed here. For the first time since Jacob died she'd begun to feel worthwhile. But, like a reflection in a house of mirrors, everything had become distorted and deranged. Tom's here now. I have to look after myself, like he does. This was her only chance to leave the village, to have his protection, to learn from him how to survive on her own. She had to go.

She quickened her step and raised her head. Four round black eyes met hers. The owls stood on the cart before her, staring straight into her guilty heart as if, in a beat, they would pluck it out. Megan's stomach twisted into a knot. She felt sick.

Just keep walking. She steadied herself. Don't turn back.

As usual Tom asked many questions while they walked to the cottage. Megan's head throbbed with such confusion that she was relieved when they reached the church and he paused to fill his pipe with dried herbs from a pouch in his pocket. She leant wearily against a tree, took off her cap and ran her fingers through her hair. The muggy heat made her drowsy. She felt she could hardly walk any further. But Tom soon set off again at a pace. When he reached the stile he noticed she was lagging behind. 'I see what she's done to you, Meg,' he said, walking back to pick up the cap she had dropped. 'I know it. Lean on me.' He took her arm and they walked on in silence.

At last they reached the cottage. Tom sat Megan down in the shade and fetched her some water. The owls approached silently. One settled on the fallen chimney bricks and the other ventured closer, perching on a bundle of hazel staves stacked against the wall. Tom saw Megan flinch.

'Gerraff!' he shouted. Fearful of the birds lunging for his eyes, he raised his arm to protect his face. He grabbed a

stone and threw it at the nearest bird. 'Leave her alone!'
Both birds screeched and flapped wildly above Tom's head
before flying off through the garden and away over the
field. Tom muttered something under his breath as he
gathered the tumbled staves.

'They'll not come back,' he growled. 'You'll be safe here.'

When Megan had rested a little she noticed that Tom had
been very busy. Apart from the large quantity of hazel he'd
cut, she saw some strange devices made of bent willow,
bound with leather thong. Here and there were piles of
stakes and nails. Tom handed Megan a bundle of twine.

'Can you untangle this for me?' he asked.

'Is it for trapping?' Megan asked as she laid out the
bundle in her lap and began to tug at the twisted loops.

'Of a kind,' said Tom. He sat under a tree, picked up a
long rod and began to whittle the end, testing the point
with his finger. 'You'll see, Meg, soon enough. I'll need you
to help me.' Megan was pleased to hear this. She intended
to make herself as useful to Tom as she could.

They worked together with little talk for half an hour.
Megan fought to stay awake, waiting for the right moment
to ask Tom if she could stay. She looked around his camp.
Would he want her here? She rolled a skein of rough fibres
between her hands, over and over, pressing until her palms
were sore, not noticing when Tom stopped to watch her.

'Why d'you do that to your hands?' he asked.

Megan felt herself flush with embarrassment. 'I just hate them, that's all. They're useless.'

A sudden wind rustled through the garden. Tom narrowed his eyes and stared at the sky. 'The weather's going to break at last. That'll bring a storm,' he said. 'Can you smell it? Let's move this lot inside.' He bent down to gather up the leather and twine in his arms, but as he lifted the bundle close to his chest he suddenly cursed and dropped it all. Tom gripped his right arm. Beads of blood bubbled up at his wrist and trickled down to his elbow.

'What was that?' He peered at the mess on the ground. Glinting among the twine was a small kitchen knife. Megan recognised it came from the Manor.

'How did that get there?' She stood up and backed away, confused.

Tom ignored her. He winced as he inspected the gash. There was a deep rip in the flesh of his forearm. He smeared the blood away with a grubby thumb.

'Tear me a bandage, Meg,' he hissed. But to his irritation she took a step further away. 'Tear us a strip of your apron. Go on. What's wrong with you?'

'I can't!' Megan cried. She began to shake. She stared at Tom's arm in terror. 'I can't help you!' She saw the blood and her head swam. She saw Jacob; his limp body, wet and choking in her arms, blood dripping through the weeds clinging to his hair, seeping from his mouth; she saw the life spilling out of him, like scarlet sap, his lifeblood smeared all over her arms, her face, as she kissed him and held him tight, the iron taste of his blood on her lips . . .

'It's only a scratch,' said Tom angrily. 'Don't be stupid. I just can't do it myself.'

'I can't!' Megan spluttered. 'You don't understand!'

The stone in her heart swelled, cramming her chest, crushing her breath away. She threw down her handful of twine. 'I can't ... I can't do it!'

'But I need you,' shouted Tom, reaching out for her sleeve. Megan pulled free.

'Come back!'

Fifteen

Storm

Megan fled. Around her the wind thrashed the trees and the sky darkened. As she reached the graveyard the storm burst. Sudden rain fell, hard and fast. Within seconds she was drenched. Megan picked up her skirts and ran, skidding between the tombstones in the long, wet grass. She darted down the church path and across the rutted track that was already filling with milky puddles. The torrent was so fierce that stones jumped and skittered around her ankles. There was only one place to go.

When Megan reached the Manor a clap of thunder

chased her through the gate. She threw herself into the kitchen and the wind slammed the door behind her.

All that afternoon the storm raged; fierce rain drummed on the roof and wind rattled the shutters as if laying siege to the house.

Megan crouched on her bed and pulled the sheets up around her head. All she could see in her private darkness was Tom's angry face.

She sat there until nightfall, shivering in her damp clothes, small and empty and utterly alone. If Marguerite rang her bell, Megan didn't hear it. At last, she curled up beneath the bedclothes and fell asleep.

Megan had a dream. She sat on a patch of bare earth in the graveyard. In her arms was a bundle wrapped in white binding. The frayed end of the bandage lay in her hand and she knew she had to unravel it. Just as she began, a distant voice called out her name. Megan gazed around the tombstones and the shadowy yews but she could see no one. Slowly she continued to unwind the bundle but her fingers became numb and clumsy. With difficulty she turned it over and over in her lap, tugging at the strips of cloth, layer after layer. Pale red speckles began to appear, blotting the white. Suddenly she realised the voice was coming from inside the bundle. Then she recognised it – Jacob's voice, muffled and faint. For a moment she paused, confused and afraid. Cautiously she continued to unwind the bandage, her hands feeling life stir in the soft, heavy parcel, then faster, drawing away long lengths that piled in a tangle in her lap and overflowed onto the ground. The binding was now damp, stained with red. The blood leeched into her hands. All the while her brother's cry persisted.

'Meggie, Meggie . . .'

But, however much she unravelled, Megan seemed no closer to reaching him. She began to panic. Turning the bundle became awkward. The harder she tried, the less she could manipulate it. She clawed at the binding but it was a struggle to move her arms. Her elbows were now pinned fast at her side. Megan couldn't writhe free, then she saw why – the long, loose lengths of bandage had been wrapping themselves around her own body. She tried biting, snatching at the cloth with her fingertips, but in her desperation she dropped the bundle, letting him fall from her useless hands. With a cry Megan woke, bound tight in the bed sheet on the floor.

At first Megan couldn't move. In the darkness she couldn't understand where she was. She rolled and twisted in the sheet. The storm pounding the thatch above her head was so loud that she wanted to cover her ears but her arms were imprisoned in the cloth. At last she loosened the sheet enough to tear herself free. Megan's hand fell upon her shawl. She grabbed it, flinging it around her head and shoulders and threw herself at the loft ladder. Half tumbling down the rungs she reached the kitchen as sheet lightning flashed through the windows. Outside, the rain-swept yard dazzled for a moment, freaked with blinding brightness, then all was dark. Rocks of thunder crashed above and the whole night shuddered. Megan grabbed the lantern, pulled her shawl tight and escaped into the storm.

Megan's only thought was to get away, from everything, from everyone. The gusting wind swept her up at once and buffeted her across the yard into the lane. She leaned into the rain and began to stagger through the mud towards East End. Once more lightning flickered and flashed to reveal a ghostly, bone-white dreamscape and then it was gone. Thunder rolled from the black belly of darkness. The faltering flame of Megan's lantern was little use as she skidded in the wet grass. Rain stung her face and whipped her hair across her eyes. Her heavy, sodden skirts wrapped themselves around her legs. Megan bowed her head into the storm and pushed on until she reached the track to the Downs.

Even the birds would not follow her in this, she thought. No one would see her. No one would know.

Megan headed up the track, dodging wind-whipped brambles and branches lashing out from the high hedges on either side. As she reached the steep rise her lantern was blown out. Megan threw it down and used her freed hand to grip the shawl tighter to her throat. She went on blindly. The wet chalk on the rise was slippery as glass. Megan slid to her knees as the slope streamed with a slurry of mud from above. She remembered that a deep quarry fell sharply from the bank somewhere near the top of the track. Keep away from the edge, she urged herself. But where was the edge in the darkness? As she felt her way around the trunk of a yew she snagged her skirt and lost her balance. All at once the ground collapsed beneath her feet and she tumbled down, crashing through gorse and nettles into the quarry below, where she fell in a crumpled heap on the hard flinty earth.

Megan screamed.

At once lightning flashed, as if drawn like a hunter to her voice. In that blinding moment Megan swung about and saw where she'd fallen. Before her rose the steep basin wall of the quarry, behind her was a deep thicket of impenetrable scrub.

Darkness.

Thunder rumbled into the pit. A havoc of twigs and leaves clattered above Megan's head. Lightning flickered again and she saw them – two silver birds at the rim of the quarry, gripping a buckled root, their feathers riffled violently by the wind.

Darkness.

Then light. The mask face of an owl stared directly into her eyes from the thicket close by. Megan picked up a stick and threw it.

Darkness.

Then light. A screech to her left. Another bird flexed its

wings and darted from the path of a falling branch.

Darkness.

Then light. A cry of pain, this time behind her. Megan twisted sharply. A white boy hovered above a thorn bush. Rain battered his fragile wings and whipped the dripping curls about his head. He stretched his thin arms towards her.

'Jaaaacob!' Megan cried.

A chaos of screeching and flapping spun around Megan's head. Through it the boy cried louder. His wail rose with the surging wind and rain. Megan reached out for him in the blackness. He was everywhere and nowhere. His desperate cry became the voice of the storm. As if he was crying the storm himself.

'I'm sorry! I'm sorry!' Megan covered her ears with her hands but the howling spectre was also the ghost in her head.

Suddenly, there was a deafening crack, as if the sky itself was rent apart. A spear of lightning struck the tall ash tree that towered above the pit, splitting the trunk in two. A great torn limb ripped away and fell over the edge of the quarry in an avalanche of smashed branches, mud and stone. Megan dropped to her knees and threw her arms across her head, as the ash came crashing down.

Sixteen

Found

A debris of broken branches littered the lane as Jack Sharpe turned his mare and cart in at the entrance of the Manor yard. But there the old horse slowed to a stop. Two owls huddled on the garden wall, pecking at something that lay between their claws. They paused and turned to face the mare. She stamped and shuffled on the threshold, then shook her mane and wilfully pulled on the halter, twisting her head away from the birds. Jack Sharpe muttered under his breath and reached for his whip. He stood up and slashed the air before them. The birds took off, unflustered, one of them snatching up a dead shrew in its beak, and made for a tall elm nearby. The farmer sat down again, shaking his head. He clicked his tongue and twitched the reins. With a snort of her steamy breath the reluctant mare entered the yard, pulling the cart behind her.

Tom stood on the bank opposite the house and watched. He glimpsed the lifeless, bedraggled figure lying among the grain sacks in the cart and ground his stick into the mud.

As the cart disappeared into the yard the owls returned, circled low and followed it in.

Megan's head ached and her whole body felt bruised and tender. She was not in the quarry, but lying in a bed, propped against several soft pillows, and she couldn't remember how she had got there. Her arms lay by her sides above the covers and a hand rested lightly upon hers. She opened her eyes. Marguerite was sitting on a chair beside the bed, fast asleep, her head tipped a little to one side. Megan slipped her hand from beneath Marguerite's fingers. She raised herself and looked around, but didn't recognise the room. There was no mistaking she was in the Manor for, like the parlour, the furniture here was disarranged and the drapes hung with cobwebs. Every surface was thick with dust. In her stupor Megan was slow to grasp what was wrong. Then she realised – shafts of morning light flooded the room. The shutters were open and the curtains drawn back. Someone had let in the light.

Megan fingered her damp clothes and muddy hair. Slowly she remembered the thunder and lightning and the quarry – but nothing else made sense. With a shiver she pulled the covers up to her chin, shut her eyes and sank back into the warmth of the bed. The movement of the bedclothes disturbed Marguerite's hand and she woke, yawning. Her fingers searched for Megan's hidden hand.

'Are you awake? Can you speak?' she whispered.

'What happened?' murmured Megan. 'Where am I?'

'You left us,' said Marguerite. 'There was a storm.' Her voice was oddly soft and apprehensive.

Everything is wrong, thought Megan. The light in the room, Marguerite, everything was different. She opened her eyes again. Specks of dust danced in the sunlight. A fly rustled inside the shade of the candlestick beside the bed.

'Jack Sharpe's dog found you in the quarry,' said Marguerite. 'Sharpe brought you here and carried you up to the nursery.'

'And you opened the shutters,' said Megan, still bewildered.

'No,' said Marguerite. 'He did.' She withdrew her hand and buried it in her lap. 'Sharpe said ...' she hesitated and sighed deeply. 'Sharpe said that if I wanted you to stay I should let in the light ... that no fair creature could live in shadows. I was wrong to frighten you, Megan, forgive me. I was afraid. I was afraid you would leave me alone again.'

To Megan's surprise, tears welled in the blind woman's eyes and she let them fall. Megan watched Marguerite

with pity and knew she would never feel scared of her
again. It was true, no fair creature could live in shadows,
but Marguerite would never wake up in the light.

For a while neither Megan nor Marguerite stirred. Distant
sheep bells clinked on the down and the sun's light and
warmth filled the nursery.

Megan drifted back to sleep. When she woke an hour
later Marguerite was gone. Megan raised herself up on the
pillows. With an effort she swung her stiff legs out of the
bed and sat on the side, feeling dizzy and weak. She shaded
her eyes to look out of the bright window. There was Tom,
standing in the lane below, staring straight up at her, the
ferret in a cage on the ground beside him. He nursed his
wrist, which was wrapped in a crude sling. When Tom saw
Megan he smiled and nodded. Suddenly she wanted to cry.
He had forgiven her. He'd been watching for her and
still wanted to be friends. She smiled back but her head
started to spin and, feeling faint, she sank down onto the
bed. Maybe he would take her with him after all. But
should she go? Tom, Jacob, the birds, the blood, the
storm, the light. Her mind was a confusion of feverish
thoughts.

But now Marguerite returned and was caring for her,
gently tucking in the covers, unpinning her own shawl
and laying it on the bed for more warmth. 'Rest,' said

Marguerite. 'Rest now. We will look after each other, you and I.'

Megan slept again but she woke shivering with a chill. Marguerite stroked Megan's forehead with her cold hand. 'You need a fire,' she said. Megan knew she hadn't the strength go out and bring wood in from the shed. She shook her head. 'Just one more blanket, please.' Marguerite left the room and did not return for some time. To Megan's astonishment, when she did come back she was carrying an armful of kindling. Megan watched the blind woman feel her way slowly towards the hearth and stumble as she knelt to lay the wood down. As Megan moved to get out of bed Marguerite raised a hand. 'Don't help me,' she said. 'I can do this.'

Four times Marguerite made her way down the stairs, out to the shed and back up to the nursery with wood. At last she allowed Megan to get up with her, to help light the fire from the lantern Jack Sharpe had left, and then she went off to fetch some clean, dry clothes. While she was gone Megan spotted the purse Tom had given her on the floor by the bed. It must have dropped out of her pocket as she was carried here. With great effort she retrieved it before Marguerite came back, and hid it under the pillow.

When Marguerite returned she brought Megan a fine overskirt and lace-trimmed underskirt, a velvet bodice, thick stockings and a moss green shawl. Megan peeled off her filthy things, scattering dried mud that rattled across the floorboards, and put the dry clothes on. Her cold fingers could hardly manage the buttons and ties but she was grateful.

As the flames crackled Megan curled into an armchair pulled close to the heat. Marguerite moved a big wingback chair beside her. 'It is many, many years since a fire burned in this room,' she said with quiet satisfaction.

A thrush sang from a treetop outside. Megan suddenly realised why the nursery was unlike any other room in the house – there was no sign of the owls. Not a feather. Not a pellet or dropping. For some reason the birds had never ventured there, or never been allowed. As if they were not permitted to prey on whatever memories were preserved in that room.

That evening Marguerite retired to the garret. Just as Megan was falling asleep she heard a low call beneath the window.

'Meg, Meg . . .'

She looked down. Tom was in the lane below, looking up expectantly, his face curiously distorted by moon shadow. Megan smiled but she drew a finger to her lips and pointed to the room above.

Tom nodded. A tiny pair of bright eyes peeped out of the neck of his smock. The ferret sniffed the night air.

'She's back, see,' murmured Tom under his breath. 'Back where I want her. We mustn't lose her again.' And, with a glance over his shoulder, he disappeared into the night.

Seventeen

Beauty

For three days Marguerite cared for Megan in the
nursery. Sometimes they sat together in silence,
sometimes in conversation and as time passed they
grew more at ease in each other's company. By the fourth
day Megan was much stronger. After breakfast Marguerite
fetched a hairbrush and they settled themselves by the
fire.

'Are you pretty, Megan?' Marguerite asked as Megan
tried to brush the residue of dried mud and chalk dust from
her tangled hair. Megan blushed at the question and smiled.
'No,' she said. 'I'm plain, like my mother.'

'Good,' said Marguerite. She raised a finger and stroked her own temples. 'I was beautiful once, you know, so people said, but beauty is dangerous. It destroys lives.'

Megan had never considered the nature of beauty before. She abandoned her hopeless task. 'Would you like me to brush your hair?' she asked. 'I could pull the chair close.'

Marguerite nodded. 'If you will,' she said graciously. 'I'm careless with it now.'

Megan knelt in the armchair and began to work on Marguerite's long, white hair. Soon she had swept it up into a fine knot at the back, fixed as best she could with the only pins Marguerite could find in her pocket.

When she was finished Marguerite examined the result with her fingertips. 'Am I still beautiful, Megan?' she asked.

Megan heard the poignant hope in Marguerite's voice. She opened her lips to tell a lie, but what she saw in the mirror made her look again. Marguerite *was*, in fact, beautiful. Her silky hair, her high cheekbones and fine skin all bloomed in the unaccustomed light and warmth. Megan realised Marguerite was not as old as she'd first thought, but probably younger even than her own mother.

Marguerite misinterpreted Megan's hesitation. 'I know it,' she said, tracing the lines etched upon her face. 'Years of sorrow have destroyed my beauty.'

'No,' Megan said. 'It isn't true.'

But Marguerite shook her head. 'What does it matter now? I no longer care what people think of me. They all flattered me long ago, until vanity made me think only of myself. It destroyed everything. Now, at least, this blindness spares me their unforgiving eyes.'

Later, as Megan sat by the fire, she thought about Marguerite's guilt, about her claim that the blindness was a punishment and her isolation in the village. Just as the new light had illuminated the house so, through their conversations, Marguerite had begun to reveal her shuttered mind. Both of them had lost something precious. Both had been rejected by those around them. Both of them were alone. Megan saw there was kindness in Marguerite's heart. Maybe they *could* help each other somehow. Burning logs hissed and shifted in the grate. If only I knew what had happened here, she thought. Maybe I could help.

Eighteen

Light

When Megan was well again Marguerite insisted she continue to sleep in the nursery.

'It will be more comfortable than the apple loft,' she said, 'and you'll not have so far to come if I need you.'

Megan agreed. Now that she was rested she realised how foolish it had been to run off that stormy night. She'd been lucky not to find herself in trouble the first time she ran away, for the whole of the south country was preparing for Napoleon's invasion. Megan had heard Tom talk of soldiers and mercenaries recruiting in the south and bands of wild men, come down from the north to look for the fight. And there were thieves, like the ones who had almost caught her on the Downs, and smugglers, working the routes up from the coast. You have to use your head, she thought. Don't move on without a plan. After all, you haven't a penny for lodgings, or a friend or relative in the world to take you in.

But Megan was no longer sure she wanted to move on, at least not so soon. She was grateful for Marguerite's care and attention while she was ill and had begun to feel some affection for her. She was also intrigued to know more about her strange companion and help her if she could. But Tom would not stay for long and Megan knew now that to be safe she needed to travel with Tom, if he would take her. She had to talk to him.

The nursery was more comfortable than Megan's mean mattress under the thatch, and a welcome sanctuary from the owls. But Marguerite's room was directly above. It would be harder to creep away unnoticed.

When Megan returned to the kitchen to resume her duties she found, to her dismay, that the room was strewn with pellets and feathers. Shrivelled entrails lay on the dishes and there were frog's legs in the salt crock. She soon spied the owls hunched close together in a deep recess of the inglenook, as if trying to pass through some small soot-black doorway from the underworld. One let out an unearthly, guttural growl as it met her eyes. The other blinked slowly and turned away. Megan almost believed they were jealous of the time she had spent with Marguerite. She pursed her lips defiantly and fetched the broom. At once the birds took flight and swooped through the open door out to the yard.

Megan had just started a fire burning in the grate when Marguerite appeared.

'Come,' she said. 'I promised Sharpe ...'

Megan followed her out of the room, curious. First they went to the parlour.

'Now,' said Marguerite, making her way cautiously among the furniture to the window. 'Help me draw the curtains.' As they gripped the heavy drapes and tugged them apart clouds of thick dust set them both coughing. Marguerite felt about for the nearest chair and sat down to catch her breath. 'Now, open the shutters.' Megan did as she was told. Light flooded the room and the true state of the disarray within was revealed. Almost at once a butterfly danced onto the sill and Megan noticed Marguerite turn her cheek to the sudden warmth.

They proceeded through every room together, doing the same. From the parlour they went to a large yellow drawing room on the far side of the hall, then up the stairs to the first floor. There, they entered a study and the morning room, where Marguerite passed the time at her bizarre embroideries. One other bedroom was also on this floor, eerily left as though the occupants would return, yet obviously unused for years. After that Marguerite led Megan up to a small galleried landing on the second floor. Here the birds had badly fouled the stairs. Megan could hardly bear the smell. She flung open a small round window and the house seemed to gasp in the fresh air. There were two more rooms at the top of the house; one filled with storage chests and old furniture; the other, Marguerite's room, in which Megan knew she would find the garret window where the birds entered and left the house. The smell at the top of the house almost made Megan retch. She held back, nervous of entering the owl room, of the sight that would meet her when she opened the door, but at the threshold Marguerite herself faltered.

'I think we'll leave the shutters here,' she said. 'I have no need . . .' Suddenly she seemed to close up and shrink away.

Megan decided, despite her apprehension, that if she wanted to help Marguerite, she had to enter the room. 'We must let in the light here,' she protested. 'The sun, the warmth . . . you can feel it.'

But Marguerite looked uncomfortable. She had shown too much. She gripped the doorframe and waved Megan away, then, without further word, she slipped into the room and shut herself in the darkness.

Nineteen

Gift

L ight and warmth transformed the Manor House and lifted Megan's spirits. Over the following days she carried a rag and pail from room to room, cleaning every surface, flinging open the windows and brushing out the dusty curtains as best she could. She heaved the rugs into the garden to beat them and found beeswax to polish the parlour table until it shone. It felt good to be busy, then to sink into her comfortable nursery bed at night. But still there was no rest in her dreams, where Jacob soared with arms outstretched, just beyond her reach.

Marguerite seemed cautious at first about the bustle of

activity around her. Like a nervous creature whose den had been disturbed, she hid away. But Megan soon caught her feeling a way around the rearranged furniture, her slim, sensitive fingers stretching like antennae into unfamiliar spaces, orientating herself, drawing a chair to the open window to savour the fresh scents of the garden beyond, or sitting where the sunlight warmed her cheek. She quickly began to adjust to the daylight hours, no longer calling for Megan through the night.

To Megan's delight, the owls retreated from the light and the fresh air that filled the house. Their familiar reek was gone; their shadows disturbed, their dark kingdom vanished. Day by day they came less often to the lower floors of the house, but Megan could still hear them scratching and tapping in Marguerite's garret room, and swooping from her window ledge into the night. Still they followed her whenever she left the house.

Megan looked out each day for Tom but, to her disappointment, he was nowhere to be seen. It was not until the tenth day after the storm that he appeared silently beside her, as she walked up to Tawks Farm.

'What have you got there, then?' he said, taking the parcel wrapped in muslin from her arms.

'Tansy cake,' gasped Megan. 'Give it me back!' She noticed with relief that his arm was no longer wrapped in the grubby bandage she'd seen from the nursery window a few days earlier, but felt momentarily shy of him.

'Hey, it's still warm.' Tom held the cake just out of her reach and took a deep breath of its honeyed scent. His eyes flashed at Megan. 'Give me a taste,' he said.

'No!' Megan took back the cake. She nestled it close and smiled at his cheek. 'It's for Jack Sharpe. To thank him.'

'You're going to thank him for taking you back there?' Tom pulled some cobnuts from his pocket, cracked them in his hand and passed one to Megan. 'I thought you were a runner. Always running away ...'

'No!' exclaimed Megan, 'It's not like that.' She slowed her step beside a fallen tree that lay in the grass. She didn't want him to think that. 'Sit here with me.'

'I'll sit for a piece of tansy cake,' said Tom, standing his ground.

Megan saw this was a test of loyalty, of friendship, and it would be the only way to make him stay. I'll make another, she thought. She sat, unwrapped the cloth and broke off a chunk of the golden cake. 'Do you forgive me?' she asked quietly as she handed it to him. 'Do you forgive me for not tending your arm?'

Tom settled himself beside her. A flash of resentment crossed his face. Then he stuffed the moist cake into his mouth and the sweetness brought a smile to his lips.

'Why did you do it, Meg?' he mumbled, helping himself at once to more. 'You're a strange one. You know that don't you?' He brushed his hand across his sticky mouth. 'See, I notice things you do. I notice everything.' He hesitated. 'But I like you.' He edged closer and picked some crumbs out of her lap. 'I can look after myself, can't I? But you could've helped me.'

Megan stared down at her hands. 'I wanted to help you, Tom. I just couldn't. I was afraid.'

'It were only a scratch,' scoffed Tom. 'All I wanted was a scrap of your skirt for a bandage.'

'I'm sorry. I just couldn't.'

'Why?'

Megan chewed her bottom lip. 'It was because of something that happened,' she said awkwardly. 'It's why I ran away.'

Tom stared at Megan with his hunter's eyes. He hunted knowledge, she thought. He preyed with his persistent questions, stalking down the one fact, the one detail that would satisfy him. Yet now she needed him to know. She needed him to trust her, to understand.

'It was because of my brother.'

For once Tom left her a silence.

'Jacob wanted to fly, you see,' she continued. 'The garden at home was steep and he was always running down, flapping his arms, pretending he was a bird. But there was a river at the bottom; I'd warned him so often that it was deep. One day the wind was strong, and he ran so fast, with his arms swooping and his feet leaping off the ground ... watching from the window I almost thought with the wind and his will and the madness of it that he just might take flight after all. Then I realised he wasn't going to slow down. He kept running, faster and faster, towards the jetty. I ran out of the house but I heard the splash before I could reach him, the screaming ...'

'Did you pull him out?' asked Tom.

Megan swallowed hard. 'There was only me, no one else was at home. I couldn't leave him to go for help. There was a boat hook . . . I dragged him towards the rushes then I jumped in myself. And when I had him on the bank, when I had him in my arms . . .' She fought back her tears. 'There was a gash in his head . . . I couldn't stop it, the blood, the life, just flowing out of him and his white face all wrapped in waterweed, staring up at me, thinking I would make it right. I pressed my hands to his head but I couldn't stop the blood, it just ran through my fingers. And then . . . then he looked faraway and was still. He was there in my arms, but he was gone.'

'You tried to save him,' said Tom softly.

'But I couldn't!' Megan clenched her nails deep into her palms. 'I told him it would be all right, but I couldn't save him. It was my fault.' She broke down and wept. And for the first time since Jacob died she cried hard and fierce, from the deep well of her grief. She cried from a place so deep it shook her heart and bones.

Tom sat without a word, shoulder to shoulder with her until all the tears were done.

When she was calm Tom gently took her hands, like an open book in his own. 'That's why you did this to your hands?' he said. Megan nodded. They looked strangely unfamiliar, small, lying in his.

'And that's why you ran away?'

Megan sniffed and dried her eyes. She nodded, remembering the grim days that followed Jacob's death. 'My parents hated me. They blamed me. Everyone blamed me,' she said. 'Three boys had died and all they longed for was a son. Then Jacob survived and everyone said he was a blessing; he was going to make everything good and when he grew up he'd take care of us all in the future. But he didn't have a future.

'When he died my parents couldn't bring themselves to look at me, or speak to me. They didn't even speak to each other. Father never came home. Mother stayed in her room. No one came to the house. Nobody. They were ashamed of me. And I knew what they were thinking. They thought it would have been better if I'd died that day instead. So many times I wished I had.'

Tom stood up. He picked up the cake and wrapped it roughly in the cloth. 'So you ran away and found yourself here,' he said. 'I reckon I'd have done the same.'

Megan sniffed and tugged at a lock of hair. She couldn't imagine him suffering any regrets.

'But listen, Meg, it wasn't your fault, do you hear me?' said Tom. 'How could you expect to save your own brother, half drowned with his head broken, when you were all alone and in a panic? Seems to me it was cruel what they did, blaming you. It was *their* fault the riverbank weren't made safe for the boy. It was their fault you were left alone. They should have blamed themselves. Maybe they did.'

Tom's words took Megan by surprise.

'No. It wasn't like that.' Suddenly she was confused. 'I saw them angry with me. I saw them turn away ...'

'But you were looking with guilty eyes,' said Tom simply.

For a moment Megan struggled with this change of perception. Could it be possible that her parents blamed *themselves* for Jacob's death? They weren't at home; it had been Cook's day off. She was left alone. The riverbank had never been made safe. Had she really misunderstood them?

Her mind struggled but her heart recognised the truth. In one beat the guilt stone that lodged there crumbled away.

'Whatever happened, you've got to make your own life now, Meg,' said Tom as they walked back towards the Manor together. 'Like me, see. You've got to believe in yourself.'

Megan turned his words over in her head. 'What do you believe in?' she asked.

Tom shrugged his shoulders and stuck his chin in the air. 'I believe in the rightness of things,' he said firmly.

Megan thought of her life. She had never known the rightness of things, only loss and despair and rejection. How could you believe in yourself without hope? And yet, she thought, Tom had set something right in her mind and her heart that day. Maybe he could help her find the rightness of things. She must learn to believe in herself now.

When they got to the gate of the yard Tom had one last question. 'Why did you go off to the Downs that night in the storm?' he asked.

'Because I wronged you,' answered Megan, 'and I was afraid. I was afraid of staying here forever, of losing myself in the shadows, like Marguerite.' She looked up into Tom's eyes, dark as glassy flint. High above them a flock of birds flew in a ragged arrow across the sky.

'Take me with you, when you go,' she said suddenly. 'I won't be any trouble. Just take me along for a while, 'til I learn how to manage in the world.'

Megan hadn't meant to ask like this. The blood pounded in her head. She waited for Tom's reaction. Suddenly everything depended on it. Tom's face gave nothing away, but his thoughts turned within, playing out some business in his head, searching beyond the one intent that had occupied his mind for many weeks. Considering, for the first time, what might come after ...

Tom scratched the back of his neck and regarded her thoughtfully then, to Megan's relief, he smiled.

'All right, I'll take care of you, Meg,' he said. 'I'll teach you how to get by. We'd have to rough it a bit at first but we could make good, you and me together.' He looked towards the Manor with narrow eyes. 'I'll not be going until All Souls, mind. I've business that night. It's not long now. Stay a while. You can help me, see. Then I'll take you with me.' He took both Megan's hands and pulled her to her feet.

'Promise?' said Megan earnestly.

'Promise,' said Tom and he stuffed the remains of the cake in his pocket.

Twenty

The Graveyard

That evening, after her talk with Tom, Megan walked up to the graveyard. Calmly now, without anger or resentment, she thought of her parents and all that had happened. If only her mother hadn't chosen to grieve alone, each time retreating further into herself, maybe they could have all helped each other; maybe Megan would have understood. For the first time she felt sad for her mother, unable to cope or ask for help, and for her father, shut out, denied, like she herself had been. And yet they must have fought their despair because Jacob was born. She saw her parents, drawn together at the cradle the day the miracle happened, almost disbelieving. Now she thought how afraid they must have been at that moment – so afraid to hope. Forgive me, she thought. I felt only my own fears and my own hurt. But she had been just a child then herself. Tom was right; she had been looking at the world through her own eyes. How could she possibly have saved Jacob that day? She couldn't have left him alone and gone for help. She couldn't have healed his wounds. Her hands were only hands ...

But I held him, I was there, she thought. And they were not. There would never be a son, never any hope for them again. Her guilt was gone and Megan felt only deeply, deeply sad.

The graveyard had seemed the best place to find Jacob. The best place to say goodbye.

She sat on a bench against the wall of the church and heard Tom's words once more. 'It's not the dead ones that won't let go, it's the other way.'

Megan gazed up above her head. 'Angel-bird,' she said softly. 'I didn't understand. I thought it was my fault and I thought you haunted me because you couldn't forgive. But now I know. I was keeping you here when all you ever wanted was to fly free. I trapped you, I broke your wings to punish myself.' She remembered Jacob before his dreams began – their games, their stories and secrets, the sound of his voice, his hand in hers. They would always be together in those memories. She picked a dry thistle and gently blew the feathery down into the air. 'Fly now, Jacob. Fly on!' The thistledown floated up and drifted away. Megan watched it dance into the distance and imagined Jacob running, flinging his arms after it ... but all she saw was the sunset rolling the day away over the hill and the still, quiet evening settling around her. Then, to her astonishment, out of the stillness, on the gentle slope of the down beyond the graveyard, a thousand larks rose as one from the tall grass. The cloud of birds fluttered higher and higher into the sky and as they flew up they began to sing. Megan watched, wide-eyed. She knew, at last, Jacob was free.

Megan stayed on in the graveyard for a while. She stopped to read the names carved on the stones. Some were too old and weatherworn to decipher, others overgrown with lichen or ivy, but as her eyes grew accustomed to the script she spelled out the words.

'Emily Davy,' she read slowly. 'Died April 4th 1785. Aged 79. Not dead but sleeping. Nathaniel Black. Beloved husband. Died aged 81.' They live long in this parish, she thought.

Then she found a younger man. Richard Percy. Aged 26. And beside him, another. Gabriel Ward. Aged 24. The graves had been long neglected. She knelt down and tried to pull the ivy off the stones but it clung fast. Without a knife it was impossible and she gave up.

But just as she was about to make her way to the gate something made her return to look again at Richard Percy and Gabriel Ward. Sure enough, her eye had caught a curious fact – both had died on the same day. She passed along thoughtfully. The next two graves belonged to more of the Ward family, Thomas and Gilbert, father and another son, both dates the same – November 2nd, 1798.

Now Megan peered at one tombstone after another in the failing light. Dread crept into her bones like a chill. She counted thirteen men, fathers and sons, buried side by side. All had died on the same day. November 2nd, 1798. All Souls Day, five years ago.

Twenty-one

Questions

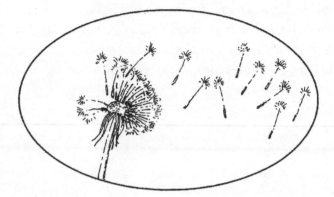

Megan was no longer plagued by dreams of Jacob, but she could not forget what she had seen in the graveyard. It was a strange coincidence – the day itself, All Souls, the day Tom was waiting for. The day he promised he would take her away.

Megan made another cake for Jack Sharpe and walked over to Tawks Farm.

As she arrived Mistress Sharpe appeared at the farmhouse door with a fair-haired child clinging shyly to her skirts. She scooped him up in her arms and he buried his face deep in her neck.

'Oh, it's you, Meg,' she said, straightening the child's breeches as he clamped his bare brown legs tightly round her waist. 'We've got a wounded soldier here. Got too close to the cooking pot and scalded himself.' She lifted the boy's calf to show Megan the burn. Megan smiled at the child. She picked a dandelion clock and offered it to the boy, but he wouldn't be coaxed to take it.

'Well, maybe not this time,' said the farmer's wife, shifting him from one hip to the other. 'Come another day, he likes company.'

I will, thought Megan, before I leave the village with Tom, I'll come back. The boy stole a glance at her once more and a smile curled his lips.

'Now, how can we help you?' said his mother.

'I brought this, to say thank you.'

'My Jack needs no thanks,' she said, unfolding the cloth a little. 'But it is his favourite.' She looked at Megan approvingly. 'You must be good for her, at the Manor, Meg. Jack told me how things have changed there.'

'Yes, he made her open all the shutters,' said Megan.

'Aye, but that's of little consequence to her.' Mistress Sharpe shook her head. 'It's your company I was thinking of.'

Megan saw her chance. 'I was walking in the graveyard,' she began. At once the farmer's wife stiffened. 'I saw thirteen graves there,' Megan continued, 'all men who died on the same day, five years ago. I wondered ...'

'We don't talk of it here,' said Mistress Sharpe abruptly. 'You'd do well to forget it.' She saw Megan's disappointed face and softened a little. 'There was an accident,' she said quietly. 'That's all you need to know. It took most of the men of the village. Most of the women too, from hard work and heartbreak after.'

'Is that why the village is so empty?' asked Megan. 'Why so many cottages are in ruins?'

Mistress Sharpe nodded. 'We lost nine farmers and hands that night. The blacksmith was killed, wheelwright and the old shepherd. Even the parson died. We had to pray over them us selves.'

'But what happened?' asked Megan.

The farmer's wife looked up at the owls, perched on the stable roof. 'There's some could tell you, if they could speak. Some as bring tragedy upon others,' she said in a low voice. 'I'll thank you from my Jack for the cake.' And she turned away hurriedly and left Megan standing alone on the doorstep.

Twenty-two

The Garden

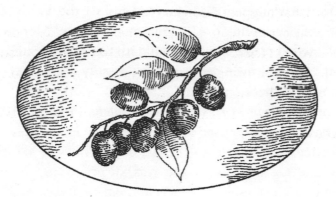

Megan's thoughts dwelled upon Tom's promise to take her away. She was filled with excitement and apprehension. The more she tried to imagine travelling with Tom the more she wished she understood him better. He was so unpredictable, so secretive. Still, she thought, there was time.

Meanwhile, she had discovered some books in the study and offered to read to Marguerite. There were volumes of poetry, romances and adventure and Marguerite listened avidly, asking Megan to repeat passages she enjoyed. When the light grew too dim to read they talked about the books together by the fire. Day by day the friendship between them continued to grow and the decision to leave troubled Megan more.

One afternoon, as Megan sat at Marguerite's feet in the upstairs parlour, sorting twists of embroidery threads that lay like shredded rainbows on the rug, she asked how it felt to live as Marguerite did – in a remembered world, conjuring visions of how things appeared.

'That is what you do as you read and see the words come to life in your mind's eye, in your imagination,' Marguerite explained. 'I read the world, but with touch and sound and scent, maybe I even sense it more keenly than you, then I imagine it before my eyes.'

The mention of scent reminded Megan of the Michaelmas daisies she'd picked earlier in the day and forgotten to bring up to the parlour. When she returned with the jug of flowers she was surprised to find that Marguerite was able to describe them perfectly, even the jug, which she recognised from the raised pattern on its belly. Megan put the flowers on the mantelpiece beside a jewellery box.

'Ah, yes,' said Marguerite, hearing the contents of the box clink as it was disturbed. She laid her needlework in her lap. 'That box belonged to my grandmother. She taught me everything that mattered. When I was young she'd take me walking in the woods to find good trees to climb and teach me the names of things, every tiny creature, every wildflower. She bought my first pony and taught me how to ride and we would gallop all day like gypsies over the Downs ...'

For a while Marguerite fell silent, drifting away on some

adventure of long ago and Megan tweaked the crimson threads from a knot of olive green and wondered where in that wild country she might be. The fire waned. Megan put down the silks and pumped the bellows to revive it. As Marguerite felt the heat flare she came to with a gasp. 'Oh, my horses!' A sudden look of anguish came upon her face and her eyes filled with tears. 'Fairwind and Caspar! My beautiful boys.' She crumpled in her chair and buried her head in her hands.

Megan watched, not knowing what to say or do. She fetched a glass of water but Marguerite would not be consoled.

At last, the blind woman rose, harrowed and red-eyed, and without another word went up to her room.

The next morning Marguerite's distress seemed forgotten.

'Are there apples in the orchard now?' she asked as Megan brought breakfast to the table.

'I haven't walked there much,' said Megan, arranging the tray before her. 'It's thick with brambles and weeds.'

'Surely the garden could not grow wild so soon?' said Marguerite. 'Time has left me without measure these past years.'

'How long since you saw it?' asked Megan.

Marguerite fell silent. Megan waited for a reply but Marguerite sat, trance-like, lost once more in her impenetrable thoughts. Megan regretted her question, although she had long wanted to ask it, and turned to leave. Just as she reached the door Marguerite mumbled something to herself.

'What is the year?' she asked aloud.

'1803,' Megan replied. 'It must be October now.'

'Then it is five years,' said Marguerite. 'Almost five years I have been blind.'

Five years. All those summers while Megan played with Jacob down by the river, those winter days she worked at her studies, all that time Marguerite had been sitting in that house, imprisoned in her darkness ...

Megan found that measure of loneliness overwhelming – it was a half-life, with no prospect of reprieve. Just endless isolation, year after year, with only the sinister, ghostlike birds for company. Why had no spinster woman come to be housekeeper? Why didn't any neighbour come to keep her company? What could Marguerite have done to make the villagers shun her?

'Tell me about the garden,' said Megan.

Marguerite raised her face as if to the sun and Megan knew she was remembering the garden as it once was, walking there again.

'The orchard and the kitchen garden were my father's pride,' said Marguerite. 'We had every sort of vegetable and fruit, bean sticks and berries, sweet herbs along the paths. He called it our little Eden.' She got up from the table and made her way across the hall to the yellow drawing room. 'There!'

Megan followed. Marguerite stood at the window with the curtains swept wide. 'Can you see it? The mulberry on the lawn and the apple trees beyond?'

144

Suddenly Megan desperately wanted to see what Marguerite saw – her Eden. She shut her eyes and heard Marguerite's words again. Slowly a glorious garden spread before her, and there stood Marguerite with her arms full of scarlet apples. Megan could almost smell their scent.

For a while the two stood together at the window, the woman with her eyes open, the girl with her eyes closed. Neither of them in the room at all.

The shriek of a jealous owl called Megan back, insisting she face the truth – that the beautiful garden was a thicket of dogwood, quickthorn and waist high weeds.

'Go out,' said Marguerite excitedly. 'Go and bring me what you find.'

Megan's heart sank but she said nothing. She went out into the wildness, determined to return with something from that garden of long ago.

Apart from a watering can and some broken clay pots Megan saw no evidence of the vegetable garden and the orchard was nothing more than a straggle of diseased trees. But, just as she was losing hope, she found a withered damson bearing six purple fruit. She gathered them in her apron and hurried back to Marguerite.

'Ah ... that's a Merryweather!' said Marguerite with delight as she tasted the damson's yellow flesh. 'Try one yourself.'

Megan bit into the purple skin. The sharp juice stung

her tongue. Marguerite laughed. 'Yes, it's best in a tart!' she said. 'But taste the summer in it. We had big, golden tarts for harvest supper, large as millstones ... or at least that's how they seemed when I was small!'

'Well, there's honey in the pantry,' said Megan, 'and the makings of pastry crust.'

An hour later she had the damsons shining like tiny suns in a pie.

Megan brought the dish to the table and Marguerite smiled at the scent of its delicious sweetness. When she had tasted it she reached out for Megan's hand. 'I am a girl again,' she said softly. 'Thank you.'

'Now, see what I found.' She pushed a large leather-bound book across the table. To Megan's surprise the pages inside were filled with watercolour sketches of the Manor House and garden, fresh and bright as if the parchment had just dried.

'Did you paint these?' asked Megan.

Marguerite smiled. 'No. My mother did. She was a fine painter. I used to watch and sometimes she'd let me mix colours for her.'

Megan studied the paintings. It was strange to see the familiar house in such beautiful surroundings. There is so much neglect here, she thought, so much that needs tending and bringing back to life. At home she could do nothing to make her parents happy, to make things right. But there, at the Manor, she could make a difference, she knew it. The garden, the house, Marguerite – who else would show them any care?

As Megan closed the book, deep in thought, a rattle of claws on the table announced the arrival of the owls.

They settled on either side of Marguerite, as if claiming a privilege.

'Do they truly speak to you?' asked Megan, as one of the birds shuffled close to Marguerite and fussed about her hair, making low murmurings in her ear.

'In their way,' Marguerite replied. She stroked the owl's head and it closed its eyes as if in a swoon.

'But how do you ... how do you see things?' Megan faltered.

'How do I see with their eyes?' Marguerite slid her hand down the length of the bird's back and it seemed to go to sleep. 'Seeing is understanding,' she said, 'and there are many ways to gain understanding – some only with the heart, but others with the senses. And when one sense no longer functions the mind sharpens the rest. I know when you have been to the graveyard, among yews, because you carry their bitter scent. I smell woodsmoke, the sweat of the boy on your sleeve ...' Megan gasped. 'The farm cat, the kitchen herbs and your fear of the birds ...' Marguerite shut her eyes. 'I hear the death watch beetle buried deep in the timbers of this old house, beating his lonely head to find a mate. I hear caution in the step of those who pass the yard and the bleat of ewes when the sheepdog slips under the stile. I hear the wind change and the winterbourne flow, and the ghosts of dead men scream.'

Twenty-three

Loyalties

'Are they always together, those owls?' Tom asked Megan as she walked with him over the down to Penbury Knoll one evening. Marguerite had retired to bed early with a headache and, to Megan's surprise, Tom had appeared, daring to tap at the door.

'Can you touch the birds?' He stooped to pick up something from the freshly dug earth outside a rabbit hole.

'Why are you so interested?' Megan stared at the scrub for a glimpse of white.

Tom rubbed the flint arrowhead with his thumb

148

and dropped it in his pocket. He turned to her. 'So can you?'

Megan sighed. She disliked talking about the owls but Tom would always persist with his questions.

'Marguerite strokes them,' she said, 'but they don't come downstairs much any more, now we've opened the shutters. They keep to the garret rooms. I'm grateful for it. The house is quite different.' She stopped to watch a pair of bullfinches flit from one blackthorn to another. 'Everything is different now.'

They continued up the chalk track towards a great ditch carved along the brow of the hill. At the sound of their footsteps the soot-faced sheep raised their heads.

Megan found the clothes Marguerite had lent her cumbersome to walk in. She had gathered the skirt up with a strip of her old muslin for a sash and turned back the long sleeves but the sash kept coming undone. As she fussed with it, Tom picked up a stone from the path.

'That's a fine crown,' he said.

'A crown?' Megan cast a glance at his hand. The bun shaped fossil was marked with a star.

'Not a crown for you, in all your finery,' he jested. 'It's a shepherd's crown, left by the faery folk for those who believe in luck. He threw the stone away across the grass. ''Spose you'll be carrying a looking glass tomorrow?'

Megan disliked the mockery in his tone and stomped on, even though the borrowed boots made her feet sore. 'Marguerite has been kind to me. She trusts me now. She knows I'll not gossip about her in the village.'

'There's no one there to gossip with 'cept those evil old rooks,' said Tom. 'Still, you must tell me everything she does, d'you hear? That's not gossiping. We can't be friends if you don't tell me what's going on. I can't help you if I don't know, can I?' Megan felt uncomfortable about Tom's demands. She felt a sense of loyalty to both Marguerite and Tom, but each seemed set against the other.

'Don't fall for her kindness,' continued Tom. 'She's only looking out for herself. She tried to keep you here by making you afraid, using those birds to menace you – now she's trying to make you like her so you'll want to stay. But remember, you're coming away with me. I'll look after you.'

'You don't understand,' said Megan. 'She's been alone a long time. Five years blind, she told me. She can't manage by herself. I can help her. I could clear a patch of garden so she could sit out a little. You should see her face when she remembers how it was ...'

'That's just how she gets you to do things for her,' Tom interrupted. 'It's like a spell.'

'But I *want* to work in the garden,' Megan said. 'It was beautiful once. She showed me paintings her mother made.'

Tom shrugged.

'Flowers everywhere and fruit trees and vegetable beds ...'

'And I s'pose she dug it all with her own pretty fingers!' Tom waved his rough hands with their cuts and scratches and torn, dirty nails.

'Why do you dislike her so much?'

'Because,' said Tom. 'Just because. And you shouldn't get too friendly either, if you know what's good for you. If you want to come away with me from this place.'

Megan understood his meaning.

They crossed the ditch and entered the shady woods. Megan watched as Tom cut himself a long hazel rod from the old coppice. Something gnawed at the guts of him like a maggot in an apple, she thought, some secret that made her afraid.

Each day she was becoming less sure of what to do. Marguerite needed her. But Tom could help her, and he'd understood about Jacob. Tom will take me away, she thought. If I don't go with him at All Souls I might be here, living a half-life like Marguerite in this place for the rest of my days ...

They emerged from the woods and climbed higher over the open grassland that was scattered with gorse and crooked blackthorns, towards the pine trees on Penbury Knoll.

'Where will we go, Tom, when we leave this place?' Megan asked. 'What will we do?'

Tom had a variety of replies to this question. He swiped his stick at a fallen pinecone and sent it bouncing down the hill. 'We could follow my brothers along the coast to Portsmouth,' he said. 'It would be a few days' walk but the weather's still fine. It'd be an adventure!' He was evidently keen on this idea.

'But what if the French come?' asked Megan. 'Isn't that

where they're gathering to fight off Napoleon?'

'There's plenty of work around soldiering men,' said Tom, as if he had lived all his boyhood years as a camp follower. 'And if old Boney makes his move and gets across the Channel, if French swords are drawn on English turf ...' he swiped at another pinecone, 'then you and I will take to the turnpike and move on, because we're free and not beholden to anyone!' He leapt onto a grassy mound and shouted: 'We'll join the gypsies!'

When they reached the top of the hill, Megan gazed at the landscape that fell away before them. She had never seen such far horizons. Tom pointed out the wild heathland to the east; Cranborne Chase, the old king's hunting grounds, to the west; and looking south, the Dorset countryside tumbling towards the sea.

His keen eyes scoured the view. 'We could take the road to Poole harbour and work our passage on ship, Meg. You in the galley and me in the crow's nest, until we reached the South Sea Islands!'

Megan laughed. 'Where do you get your stories from?'

'Father's brother was a drover. He collected beasts from farms far about and walked them to market. He brought back tales from all around.'

Megan sat down beside him. 'Tell me about your mam and dad,' she said.

'There's nothing to tell,' replied Tom. 'We rubbed along as folk do until Father died, then Mam had eleven of us to feed.'

'How did she manage?'

'Well, she sent the two girls away, to work as kitchen maids in town,' said Tom. 'They'd been going on about being old enough to leave – always moping around. I heard them say they were after finding husbands, but I can't see as anyone would want them, they're both daft as moon-calves Mam always said.

'The four boys went off soldiering.' He spat into the scrub. 'They were keen for it too. Sent back good money, although Mam didn't think it all came from soldiering. That just left me and our four little 'uns.'

'Where did you live?' asked Megan. 'You know this country but I thought you didn't come from round here?'

'I never said where I was from,' snapped Tom. 'I just said I was passing through.' He caught a flash in Megan's eye. 'Mam took us to live with our Gramma, not far, over Chettle way.' He nodded towards the western hills. 'It was a squeeze. I had to sleep at the neighbour's. The old man there was on his own. Mam took in washing and had to care for Gramma too and without the girls to help. Her legs gave her pain and she was plain worn out in the end, but she didn't shirk or complain. She never gave up on getting by.'

Megan guessed that Tom had inherited some of his mother's strengths. 'What about your father?' she asked.

Tom scuffed his boots in the pine needles, then he lifted his eyes and stared at something Megan couldn't see.

'Fire!' he hissed. 'Fire killed him.'

'What happened? Was there an accident?'

'It weren't no accident,' said Tom darkly.

They sat in silence after that, watching the scarlet sun sink through rippled ranks of copper cloud.

'It's time to be going,' said Megan at last. But Tom

wouldn't move or speak. She waited a while longer but he remained still and silent as stone.

So she left him on the knoll and walked off alone towards the down. As she reached the edge of the wood Megan stopped to look back. There, on the brow of the hill was the black figure of Tom, standing against a sky of flame.

Twenty-four

Words

The days were still warm and Megan set to, clearing the woods from the little redbrick yard outside the kitchen. She brought a wicker chair and table from the yellow parlour, putting them in the sheltered nook of the house, and found a walking stick in the passage so that Marguerite wouldn't stumble on the uneven ground. Marguerite was delighted to be able to sit outside and stayed for hours at a time. She seemed unaffected by the chill of autumn mornings, or the creeping mist of dusk.

Sometimes Marguerite would ask Megan to pick her a bough or stem from the garden so that she could handle it, feeling the texture of bark and leaf, turning nuts and berries between her fingers like precious jewels. One evening she sat still for so long that Megan found a spider's web trembling between the lace of her sleeve and the whip of a briar rose nearby.

It was on one such evening, after she had fallen asleep in her chair that Marguerite was woken by a noise in the yard. Logs shifted in the woodshed.

'Megan?' But she knew at once the furtive sound was not the girl fetching firewood. From somewhere nearby came a rasping screech. Reaching for her stick Marguerite stepped cautiously through the archway into the yard. A pair of white feathers fluttered like lost snowflakes to the ground.

'Who's there?'

Tom stepped out from the woodshed. The owls were making wide swoops of the yard in alarm, working the air urgently with their broad wings, carving arcs around him. They sensed Tom's fear and swung close with talons hanging low. Tom raised an arm across his face to protect himself. When they saw Marguerite both birds came to rest on the old plough beside her. They swayed warily, dipping and ducking their moon-like faces, agitatedly pecking at the air. Then one bird raised its head and shrieked, ripping the silence apart.

'So, it's you.' Marguerite recognised the reek of pipeweed and ferret. 'The one who watches. Yes, I hear you watch. She never sees you but I know you're there. Who are you?'

Fear and fury burned in Tom's blood.

'Allen.' He thrust the word at her as if it were a weapon. 'Tom Allen.'

Marguerite stepped away gripping her stick with white knuckles. 'Megan!' she called towards the house.

'She's not there,' said Tom quietly. 'She's gone to pet Sharpe's child.'

'Megan!'

'I tell you, the girl's gone.'

'You've no business here, Tom Allen,' said Marguerite.

'But I have.' Tom stared right into her blind eyes. 'You know I have.'

'What do you want?'

'I want a reck'ning,' said Tom. 'And then things will be settled.'

'There's nothing to be done, now,' said Marguerite. Her voice faltered and her breath grew short. 'It was long ago. What's to be gained ... ?' But the thud of footsteps across the yard told her he'd left, not waiting to listen to her words.

When Megan came home from Tawks Farm later that evening she found Marguerite collapsed at the bottom of the staircase, her breath shallow and her legs all awkward beneath her.

'What happened?' gasped Megan. 'Did you fall?'

Marguerite shook her head. She leant against the wall, eyes shut, her face ashen and her thin limbs trembling. Megan saw at once that she was unable to stand. She fetched a rug and wrapped it around Marguerite then she took both hands in hers. They were icy cold. Megan sat close and held them to her own warmth. She worked her hands, rubbing warmth and life into those fingers, deathly cold.

'Are you hurt?' Still Marguerite wouldn't speak. Gently Megan touched her arms and legs, her ankles, but nothing was broken. Slowly Marguerite's breathing settled and colour reached her cheeks. Megan drew back the veil of silver hair that had fallen across her face and pinned it up. 'Shall I bring you something?' Marguerite nodded towards the garret room. 'Take my arm,' said Megan and together they climbed the stairs. When they reached the top floor landing, Marguerite would not let Megan enter the room. She clasped her collar tight to her throat.

'Lock the doors!' she hissed urgently, huddled like a woman twice her age, then she stepped inside and snapped the latch behind her.

Twenty-five

Doubt

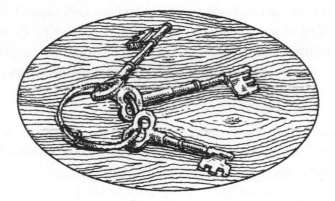

Marguerite did not come out of her room again that day. Megan sat outside the door, wondering whether to leave her alone or go in against her wish. Two hours passed and Megan knocked gently at the garret door. She heard the rustle of birds' wings, their claws skittering on the floorboards and something was knocked over.

'Shall I bring you supper?' Megan put her ear to the door. The owls scratched at the other side and hissed. She knocked again and raised her voice. 'Are you unwell?'

'There is nothing to be done,' said Marguerite faintly.

'What happened?' Megan took hold of the latch but a commotion of beating feathers made her hesitate.

'Leave me be,' said Marguerite. 'You are kind and good, Megan. But you must go away now, flee this place. Get away, it is time for you to go.'

Megan went out into the evening and paced the yard. Something dreadful had occurred, she knew. Marguerite had never bidden her lock the doors before. And why should she tell Megan to leave when she needed her? She looked up at Marguerite's window. The birds were not at their usual perch on the ledge. They were probably at her side. But what use were they to Marguerite? I cannot leave her now, thought Megan. I won't run away again.

Maybe she could persuade Tom to stay a while longer instead. If only he didn't dislike Marguerite, he could be helpful at the Manor. She set off up the village.

She came to the hedge at the back of the garden and was about to stoop through when she saw Tom, crouching behind a bush. He was staring intently through a gap in the branches at a bird trap beyond. The crude cage stood endways up and attached to the top of it was a piece of string; the other end lay in his hand. On the ground in front of it Tom had scattered crumbs of Megan's cake, which, she guessed, he must have saved for the purpose. A sparrow had spotted the crumbs and started to follow the trail. Megan held her breath as she watched it hop closer and closer to the trap. Then with a jerk of the string the cage fell. Tom had his supper. He darted forward to snap its neck and then added it to a small bulging bag he had hidden inside his jacket.

Megan stepped through the hedge and he spun round.

'How long have you been there?' he said sharply.

'Just long enough to watch you catch the bird.' Megan, already feeling shaken, was taken aback by his unfriendly eye. 'I could bring you some bread tomorrow. It wouldn't really be stealing.'

'Keep your bread,' said Tom, winding in the string. 'We'll take it with us when we go.'

'But when will we go?' asked Megan. 'Is it soon?' Tom ignored her and gathered up his trap. He started back towards the cottage and she began to follow him. But he stopped and turned.

'Go away, Meg,' he said firmly. 'I've things to do.'

His silent figure in the dusk suddenly frightened her.

'I need to talk to you,' she said. 'Something has happened ...' His only answer was to stab his stick into the ground, hard and urgent. She backed away.

'It's nearly done now. Tonight is All Souls' Eve.' Tom's voice was cold and full of foreboding.

Megan didn't understand why he'd changed. What had happened to him? First Marguerite, now Tom both sending her away. Climbing back through the hole in the hedge she picked up her skirts and ran.

When she returned to the Manor Megan listened again at Marguerite's door but still there was no sound. Maybe she's asleep now, thought Megan. Maybe this will pass, like one of her strange trances and she'll not even remember it tomorrow. I'll be here. I won't leave her.

As she lay in bed Megan couldn't get Tom's voice out of her head, telling her to go away.

'All Souls' Eve,' she whispered to herself as her heavy eyelids closed. Would Tom still come for her? What should she do?

That night Megan dreamed she was up among the pine trees on top of Penbury Knoll, hunting for Tom. She could hear him chanting close by. 'Meg, Meg, it is almost done.' His voice seemed to come from everywhere and nowhere. She ran in and out of the trees, ducking low branches, skidding on the slippery needles, chasing after shadows. Then she found a trail of crumbs scattered on the ground. 'Don't follow,' she warned herself as she caught her breath. Yet she could not resist. Step by step she walked deeper into the dark wood. A sudden wind shook the trees. Megan looked up. It was no natural weather but the wind of the wings of a hundred white owls, perched in the canopy above. The birds began to shriek and the noise was unbearable.

'Tom! Tom!' cried Megan but she knew he would never hear her above the terrifying din. She fell to the ground and buried her head in her arms.

When Megan woke Marguerite was standing at her
bedside. She gripped the bedpost, pale as death.

'They've gone!' she uttered. 'My birds. They've gone.'

Twenty-six

All Souls

'What happened?' Megan asked, reaching for her clothes and pulling on her stockings.

'It happened in the night,' said Marguerite with a trembling voice. 'Didn't you hear?'

The dream! Of course Megan had heard the birds. 'But how do you know they're gone? Maybe they'll return later.'

'They are gone, I know it,' said Marguerite. 'They were taken. I heard them, fierce and frightened.'

'But what would take them?' asked Megan. 'A buzzard? A fox?'

'You must search everywhere,' said Marguerite. 'Bring

them back to me, or tell me what you find – no matter how
. . . distressing . . . I must know what has happened to them.'

'I'll go,' said Megan, seized with terror at having to
search for the birds and the thought of what she might
find. 'But while I am gone rest here, in my bed. It's still
warm and you are not well.' Marguerite did not resist.

'Just go – and return soon. I cannot rest until they are
found.'

Megan searched the garden, the yard and the outbuildings
for signs of the birds. All she found were two white feathers
lying on the ground outside the woodshed. There seemed
to be no sign of struggle or attack. How far did the owls
fly when they went hunting at night, where did they go?
Megan was used to them following her silently around the
village but she guessed their natural territory was wide. She
remembered once seeing them quarter the fields behind the
house and decided to look there.

All morning Megan peered into derelict barns and
abandoned cottages. She scoured the woods and hedgerows
and walked up the west lane to the foot of the down. I've
no hope of finding two birds here, she thought as she

scanned the open grassland spread before her. Tom would know where to look. But she couldn't ask for his help – he hated the birds, he was terrified they would scratch his eyes out and, anyway, she wasn't sure he'd want to see her after sending her away so strangely the night before. Suddenly she realised what day it was ... All Souls! November 2nd. The day Tom was moving on. Was that why he'd been so harsh with her? Maybe he had changed his mind and decided not to take her. Maybe he'd already gone to the Manor and she wasn't there! Megan forgot about the birds and hurried back to the village. Now, she thought, as she ran down the lane, now I must decide. If it isn't too late ... if I haven't missed Tom. Should she take her only chance, could she leave Marguerite and go?

Megan reached the end of the lane out of breath. She stopped and pulled off her boots so that she could run faster. Her heart pounded, her mind raced. She imagined Marguerite lying ill in the nursery bed, alone, fretting over the owls. But she didn't really need the birds, thought Megan. They were grim companions, creatures of prey that belonged in the wild. She needed human companionship. If only there was someone to befriend Marguerite it would be easier to go with Tom. I can't stay here, Megan told herself. I *have* to go. She kneaded her hands together. But I *can't* leave her like this ...

Where was Tom's rightness of things now?

When Megan reached the Manor there was no sign of Tom and no way of telling if he had already been for her. Megan steadied herself and crept up to the nursery. Marguerite was asleep but restless. She rolled her head on the pillow and muttered words that Megan could not understand. Every now and then she cried aloud, opened her blind eyes and threw her arms out towards some imagined figure before her, whether bird or man Megan couldn't tell. Then she buried her head and her thin body heaved beneath the covers.

Megan took Marguerite's hands in hers. Almost immediately the blind woman became calm. To Megan's astonishment her breathing grew quiet and she lay still. Megan felt the bond of trust, of affection between them, easing Marguerite's distress. She looked at the hands that could not save Jacob, the hands she had cruelly punished. These hands have brought warmth and light into this dark, cold house, she thought, and now they are bringing comfort to Marguerite. Maybe I've been wrong about them; about myself. How much more could I do if I really believed?

Megan shut her eyes. No matter what happens, I have to help her now. She rooted her stockinged feet to the floor, to the stillness of the earth far below, the deep white bones of the chalk, the dark secret flint within. All her being, her sensibility, her will to help Marguerite, flowed like sap into her hands. Thought slipped away. Time slipped away.

Megan had no idea how long she stood at Marguerite's bedside before the smell of smoke broke her trance. For a moment she was confused – there was no fire in the grate, no pot cooked dry on the hearth below. Then alarm gripped her. She ran to the window. A flurry of cinders floated over the roof. The crack and spit of burning wood exploded close by – it must be in the farmyard.

Megan flew down the stairs into the kitchen. Through the window she saw grey smoke billow above the garden wall.

She ran through the archway into the yard. There, blazing before her, was a fierce bonfire, tall as a man, spitting and hissing and spewing spiralling columns of smoke. Around the fire a makeshift barricade of hurdle fences had been tied together and beside it stood Tom, wearing a grotesque wicker mask that completely covered his head like a helmet, with slits for his eyes and a gash in the weave at the mouth. On his hands were huge gauntlets that looked like they'd been made from his jerkin. He held a long wooden pole with a hook screwed into the end of it and was staring up at a cage that hung from a crude gibbet, high above the flames. Inside the cage, a heaving shape beneath a leather hood rocked from side to side. Megan tried to shout but was struck dumb, as if in a nightmare. She watched, paralysed, as Tom poked the pole between the bars of the cage, snagged the hood and drew it up, off the birds. The owls were terrified. They shrieked and thrashed from side to side, crushing their wings in the cramped space as they tried to flex them. Megan ran forward, shielding her face from the heat. Tom swung round and she stopped in her tracks. His eyes burned like embers through the slits in the dark mask.

'What are you doing?' screamed Megan. 'Tom – what have you done?'

'Stay back,' Tom raised his pole between them. His voice growled low and strange, his throat parched from the heat. Megan staggered back. What had possessed him?

'Get them down!' She shouted above the birds' frenzy.

'Stay out of this,' warned Tom. 'I've no business with you here now. I've waited a long time for this. Go fetch her.' He coughed and spluttered with the smoke, raised his mask a little and spat into the fire.

'You know she cannot come!' gasped Megan. 'She is sick. Sick with worry for the birds.' Megan looked around helplessly. Had no one else seen the fire or heard the screams?

'Why did you take them? What are you doing?'

'Bring her down here,' said Tom. 'Ask her what happened on All Souls. Ask her what she did, five years ago.'

'She can't stand. She's sick. Let her be.' Megan pleaded with him. 'I saw the graves, Tom. Tell me what happened.'

Tom planted his staff at his heel and looked up towards the garret window. '*She* killed my father,' he snarled. '*She* killed him, and others too.'

'It's not true!' cried Megan.

'It's true, I tell you!' Tom shouted angrily. 'There was a fire in the yard. The ricks caught it. She sent the men in to the burning barn and the roof collapsed on them. Thirteen died. She made nine widows.'

'But why?' The smoke was blown in Megan's face. She choked and rubbed her smarting eyes. 'Why would she do that?'

'To save her horses!' Tom shouted above the owls'

desperate cries. 'When the barn caught fire they were trapped inside. Every man was struggling to save the farm, but all she cared for was her horses. She sent the Squire, her father, into the barn to fetch them, but he never came out. Then she sent the hands and neighbours in after him.'

Megan felt sick. All became suddenly clear – the graves, the devastated village, the bitterness of the people who remained.

Tom shouted angrily, 'Ask her, I said! Bring her here.'

Megan backed away. The fire dazzled the darkening sky, leaping up almost high enough to lick the cage of birds suspended above. Gold lights and flickering shadows danced upon the long thatched wall close by. A plume of sparks cascaded towards it.

'Tom!' screamed Megan. 'Put out the fire – you'll catch the thatch! Fetch down the birds!'

'The fire must burn and I'm not done yet,' cried Tom. 'Fetch her!'

'But what are you *doing*? This won't bring them back! You told me to let go – you were right. You can't make good like this.'

'I'll do what I must!' Tom shook his stick as a threat now. 'She owes it!'

Megan saw it was no use arguing. She looked at the bucket by the well but the fire burned with a ferocious white heart. There was nothing she could do on her own. She had to get help. She turned and ran out of the yard.

Twenty-seven

The Reck'ning

Tom turned back to stoke his fire and his anger.

Moments later a frail figure stepped through the archway into the yard. Marguerite stumbled back against the wall, recoiling from the heat of the blaze. She raised her arms to shield her face and dropped her walking stick.

'Give me the birds!' she cried.

Her voice could not be heard above the roar of the flames and the din of the terrified owls, yet Tom felt her presence at once. He had waited for it. Willed it. He spun round on his heel.

'Give me the birds!' cried Marguerite again. She knelt down and felt about for her stick, then raised herself with difficulty to her feet once more.

Tom didn't move. He stood beneath the gibbet. The cage swung wildly as the birds, hearing Marguerite's voice, struggled more desperately above.

'Come and get them,' shouted Tom, 'or are you afraid? There's no one here to walk into fire for you this time. They're all gone, you saw to that. All gone ... thirteen fathers and sons, but not parted in peace.'

Marguerite turned to his voice and started to make her way towards him.

'Listen to them scream,' he taunted. 'Did you hear them scream that night when fire fell upon them?'

Marguerite tapped her stick before her, stepping cautiously over the cobbles and weeds, determined to reach the birds. 'I never meant for anyone to die,' she said, reaching out her hand. 'I lost my father too ... I never ... I just ...' Her voice faltered. She stopped and swayed. The reek of smoke, the blistering heat, the sizzle and crackle of the blaze, the screams ... it was happening again. That night. The chaos. Confusion. She swung round. Everyone in the village had come to help. There were the men taking up pitchforks to drag the burning hay from the ricks, shouting to each other, sweat streaming, skin scorched as they beat the flames. There were women, choking into their aprons, swinging pails of water from the well, hand to hand, but it was little use. Children cried, dogs barked and the beasts tramped, terrified in their stalls. She saw her father working desperately with the men, fear blazing in his eyes.

Then his anger as she pleaded with him to save her horses.

'Get away! I'll not risk men for beasts. It's all hands to save the farm.'

'If you'll not go for them I'll go myself!' Once more she felt the heat as she ran for the barn, the thunder of hooves, the panic of the horses inside ... Suddenly she was thrust to the ground and she heard her mother scream.

'NO!'

Marguerite could only watch, desperately praying for them to emerge from the flames – but nothing, no one came out.

Then she'd gripped Jem Allen's arm, crying frantically. 'The Squire – he's in the barn!' At once he'd shouted to the other men and they threw down their rakes and followed him inside.

A moment later there was a deafening crack and thunder of combustion as the rafters burned through and the vast, blazing roof fell in.

Marguerite heard one scream above the rest.

'Help!' Tom struggled to push the mask off his head. 'Get me out! I can't get out!' The gibbet had fallen, flinging the cage clear of the fire but plunging its length right into the heart of the flames. It had smashed away a heap of flaming timbers that collapsed on Tom's legs, knocking him to the ground. Tom gripped the mask that thrust his head

173

back awkwardly. He dug his elbows in the ground to heave himself free of the fire but the weight on his legs was too heavy and he couldn't feel his feet at all.

Marguerite heard Tom's screams and she knew. He had fallen. He was burning. But she also heard the birds, their screeches muffled as one bird lay upon the other, close to the ground now – maybe within her reach. She fell to her knees and began to crawl across the yard, coughing and shaking, dragging herself fist by fist.

Twenty-eight

Saved

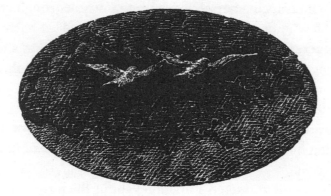

It was almost dark when Jack Sharpe arrived with Megan in his cart just as flames started to roll along the ridge of the thatched wall towards the lowest eaves of the house. He jumped down, reached for his rake and began to pull the burning straw away.

The bonfire itself was almost wasted. Megan ran towards the heap of glowing embers. She stared at the fallen hurdles and smouldering gibbet, then in the flickering light she saw them – two figures, lying close to each other in the grass. Tom's feet and legs were badly burnt, Marguerite's bare arms charred black with smoke. Neither moved. The grim mask lay close by, grinning at the devastation.

As Megan rushed to them she heard Tom groan. He stretched out to touch his legs but sank back, writhing with pain. Marguerite raised her hand towards Megan. 'Help him,' she said hoarsely. 'Help the boy.'

'What happened?' cried Megan. 'I don't understand.'

'It's done.' Tom spat the words through clenched teeth. 'Fire fell on me. She pulled me free.'

Megan helped Marguerite sit up against the trough close by. She untied her shawl and wrapped it around Marguerite's shoulders, then turned to Tom's burnt shins. Tearing strips off her skirt she gently bound them both. He screamed and gripped her arm.

'It'll be all right, Tom, I'll look after you this time,' she said, pushing the sweat sodden hair from his brow and holding him close. 'It's all over.' She raised his head gently on her lap.

Marguerite muttered something about the birds.

Megan couldn't make sense of what had happened.

'How did you come here?' she said. 'You were so ill.'

'I heard the birds call,' said Marguerite. 'I found strength somehow and I walked.' Megan stared down at her hands covered in ash and blood and blinked back her tears.

'It is over.' Marguerite sighed deeply.

Tom heaved himself up until he was sitting beside Megan.

'Is this what you were waiting for, Tom? Why did you do it?' she asked.

'I don't know.' He sounded drained, bewildered. 'I never meant to kill the birds. I just knew I had to settle things. I had nothing else since Mam died – just this reck'ning. It was all I had left, all I owned.' He turned with difficulty towards Marguerite but wouldn't raise his eyes to look at her. 'A life saved for a life taken,' he mumbled. 'That's some settling of things.'

Marguerite nodded. Her face was smeared with dirt and tears. 'Some settling,' she said. 'Maybe we can both live now, Tom Allen. We owe it to those who are gone.' She gazed blindly about the yard. 'What happened to the birds? I can't hear them anymore.'

Megan looked around for the cage. It lay beside the gibbet, the door broken apart but not a bird or feather in sight. 'They've flown,' she said.

'So then, it really is ended.' Marguerite raised her face to the sky. 'They came to this place the night of the fire. Almost as if they were conjured from the flame and smoke itself. They were the last sight I saw before the blindness came upon me. Then they were all that remained.'

The owls, of course. At last, in the embers of Tom's reckoning, Megan started to understand. There were always birds, she thought. Two men, the Squire and Tom's father both killed in the fire. Marguerite haunted by her guilt, Tom fixated with his rightness of things. Maybe now two more souls could pass on in peace.

'I no longer need the birds, Megan,' said Marguerite. 'I don't need their eyes. You have healed me.'

Tom squinted through his pain at Marguerite.

'You have brought me back to bright places,' she continued. 'You've reminded me of what endures that is good. I was not only blind in my eyes but in my heart and mind. I see now, I see what matters. It is enough.'

Megan felt something unfamiliar stir inside her own heart. It felt good. It felt like something to believe in.

Rain began to fall – not a passing spit and drizzle, but a purposeful downpour, cold and hard. It extinguished the last breath of fire with a hiss of steam. On the other side of the yard Jack Sharpe stopped soaking the thatch with buckets of well water and sheltered in the doorway to catch his breath. Megan turned to Tom. She could no longer see his face in the darkness but she knew it really was over. They could all come out of the shadows now; the ghosts of the past were gone. Grief and guilt were ashes in the fire. She slipped from his side and knelt beside Marguerite, raising her hands before Marguerite's face. Rainwater streamed down her palms – they trembled, every nerve alive. 'I can do more,' she whispered. 'You will see. I can do more ...'